ETERNITY

The Best Romance from Vietnam

KIEU BICH HAU

Ukiyoto Publishing

All global publishing rights are held by

Ukiyoto Publishing

Published in 2025

Content Copyright © KIEU BICH HAU

ISBN 9789370094420

All rights reserved.
No part of this publication may be reproduced, transmitted, or stored in a retrieval system, in any form by any means, electronic, mechanical, photocopying, recording or otherwise, without the prior permission of the publisher.

The moral rights of the author have been asserted.

This book is sold subject to the condition that it shall not by way of trade or otherwise, be lent, resold, hired out or otherwise circulated, without the publisher's prior consent, in any form of binding or cover other than that in which it is published.

www.ukiyoto.com

For HJB, with my great love and gratitude

Contents

CHAPTER ONE	1
BUDAPEST FLAME	1
CHAPTER TWO	14
NIGHT BUTTERFLIES IN HA NOI	14
CHAPTER THREE	22
THE WOMAN ON THE HILLTOP	22
CHAPTER FOUR	32
TRAVEL IN MEMORY	32
CHAPTER FIVE	46
THE DICHOTOMY OF LOVE	46
CHAPTER SIX	59
AN ORGANIC MARRIAGE	59
CHAPTER SEVEN	72
THE SPECTRAL MAP OF JANOS HILL	72
CHAPTER EIGHT	92
ON HEAVEN'S HILL	92
CHAPTER NINE	103
AT THE BOTTOM OF ECSTASY	103
CHAPTER TEN	117
JAMES BOND'S TEARS	117
CHAPTER ELEVEN	128
BLUE FOOTPRINTS	128
CHAPTER TWELVE	141

IN THE HEART OF BUDAPEST	141
CHAPTER THIRTEEN	149
MEDITATION AT VYSEGRAD	149
CHAPTER FOURTEEN	153
SOLACE OF THE FOREST NIGHT	153
CHAPTER FIFTEEN	164
RETURN TO ETERNITY	164
About the Author	175

CHAPTER ONE
BUDAPEST FLAME

Leaning backward, An fastened her seatbelt with two slender fingers and gently tightened it, then closed her eyes, taking a deep breath. In the moment, everything felt unchangeable. The plane was about to take off, journeying from Hanoi to Budapest, with a transit at a Russian airport. A flight lasting almost a day and night. An had a fondness for flights, and it would upset her if she went a whole month without boarding a plane and skillfully pulling her seatbelt with those elongated fingers at least once. But this time was different; this flight could be fateful, forever altering the course of her life. A life that she had designed and led herself without any hesitation.

Yet, she challenged herself inwardly. Would she remain true to herself?

Had she grown and matured? Or was she merely deceiving herself, pursuing the call of her rebellious heart like a naive and whimsical girl?

With her eyes closed, she drifted away from her external self, diving deep into the depths of her soul, seeking honesty.

Without a doubt, she longed for Andras. When he left Hanoi for Budapest, sleep eluded her. The subsequent nights were spent restlessly in bed, consumed by thoughts of him. He became a distraction, interrupting her profound musings during work. She loathed herself for being so consumed by him, for losing her cool and acuity. Such a state was unacceptable for someone known as the literary wizard—the luminary of romantic short stories, an independent journalist unapologetically advocating for gender equality, a charming woman with a demeanor as gentle as water, yet unyielding against any attempts to manipulate or ensnare her, no matter how tempting the offers. No man could possess her, no matter how cunning and devious they were. She always escaped the trickiest of circumstances. An aesthete who worshipped freedom, content with her single life and adoring of its independence.

The plane roared into the sea of clouds as her thoughts of Andras turned as hazy and opaque as the mist. The queen of equanimity within her emerged, propelling her forward. She turned on the screen in front of her seat, selecting a captivating movie to watch. "A Star is Born," with its mesmerizing soundtrack, love, and remorse, swept her away, evoking tears of compassion. She watched

the movie again and again, her eyes swelling with the tears she shed. The emotions evoked by the film, mingled with her suppressed affection for Andras, had set free the flow of tears from her heart.

The project of designing new software for major German corporations and offices inundated Andras with an abundance of work. Day and night, he toiled under the weight of pressure. A celebrated poet in a country where the Danube river meandered romantically, yet he earned his living in the world of IT. He was an enigma, a fusion of contrasting energies—a poet and a mathematician, a spiritual speaker—all with exceptional talents. In this very moment, he worked overtime, yearning for a prolonged getaway with An in Budapest. However, he couldn't dare believe that An would traverse over ten thousand miles from Ha Noi to Budapest just to see him. Anxious, worried, hopeful, and skeptical, he found himself caught in an emotional whirlwind. He couldn't find peace. And in the end, like many times before upon returning to Budapest, he surrendered, letting himself drift back to Ha Noi on that fateful morning of the Nguyen Tieu festival.

The first time he set foot in this enchanting Southeast Asian country was at a poetry festival in Quan Gio. Andras immersed himself in the ambiance, listening to international poets perform amidst the gentle Spring drizzle. The air was redolent with the earthy scent of soil and the fresh aroma of budding tropical spring flowers, with raindrops dancing in the air, now shining, now hidden by the sun. Poetic verses, melodies of music, and the chorus of human voices intermingled, captivating his senses. Occasionally, his attention wandered, but he made an effort to refocus on the renditions—a strange tumult within him.

The festival venue was adorned with an abundance of vibrant flowers, with red stripes and magnificent costumes adding to its allure. The person who had been sitting next to him had already left, but he left a book of poetry on the chair as if to claim the spot, uncertain if the person would return or not.

Suddenly, a soft and charming voice cut through the bustling sounds of music and conversations. "Hi, may I sit here?" a melodic voice asked.

"Of course," Andras replied, looking up and lifting the book of poetry, only to be taken aback by the radiant smile on her face. "Didn't we meet last night?"

"Yes, we did. You are the Hungarian poet," she affirmed.

She nodded gracefully and settled down beside him. Andras couldn't help but steal glances at her attractive and poised face, and in that moment, a ray of Nguyen Tieu sun filtered through a fissure in the rainproof canvas of the stage, causing her eyes to gleam. His heart skipped a beat, and he yearned to preserve this fleeting moment in the depths of eternity.

The night before, serendipity had placed him close to her at a banquet hosted by the organizers of the International Poetry Festival. It felt almost magical, as if that lone chair had been waiting just for him. Though he couldn't recall their conversation, he vividly remembered the sumptuous feast and the buoyant ambiance that enveloped them. He wished the night would never end, but they were eventually whisked away by others, and in the midst of it all, he had forgotten to ask her name. Now, fate had given him another chance to rectify what he had missed.

"May I know your name? I would like to present you with this poetry collection," Andras spoke earnestly, taking out a pen to inscribe her name in Vietnamese from the name card she had handed him.

Amazement struck him once again when he noticed that she was a writer, and her name shared a part of his own. It felt like a divine design, as if the universe itself conspired to bring them together.

"For An, with all my heart," he inscribed on the book, offering it to her with a smile.

Reading his dedication, she appeared puzzled, but soon a smile graced her lips, and she said, "Your signature is so special. It looks like the S shape of Vietnam."

His journey to Vietnam had begun out of curiosity, with the intent to learn about this intriguing land. However, the vibrant and electrifying atmosphere of the airport and bustling streets, coupled with the glimmer in An's eyes, captivated him beyond measure. He wanted to stay as swiftly as he had arrived, embracing a harmonious intersection of time and space that fueled his boundless mobility as an extraordinary IT expert, traversing time and space to create his own captivating universe.

***

With An's suitcases in his arms, Andras reached for the key to his apartment. However, a sudden wave of confusion washed over him as he stood before the door.

"Is something wrong?" An inquired curiously.

"I made a mistake. This isn't my apartment. Mine is one floor up. Oh my God! I've never mistaken my own home like this before!" he exclaimed, his composure shaken.

Andras turned away, leading the way to his correct unit. An followed him, a knowing smile on her face. She had won, causing him to lose his way right at the entrance to his own condo. The mathematician had momentarily lost his sense of direction, transformed into a poet, adrift even at the door of his own home.

Upon entering his apartment, An was utterly astounded by the vast universe of books that lay before her. Her eyes delved deeply into the living room, where shelves reached all the way up to the ceiling, neatly stacked with books. Some parts of the shelves were even shaped like a guitar, seamlessly blending with a bench, a bunk bed, and a corridor, creating an aesthetic and intellectual space. It was a vibrant library housed within a creative living environment—something she had always desired but had never fancied she would encounter. And yet, there it was, right before her eyes, and she could scarcely believe it was real.

"What a heavenly place!" An exclaimed with unbridled excitement. "How did you manage to create such a spectacular space?" she asked, finally formulating her question.

"Here," Andras pointed to his head, a gentle smile on his lips, "with the collaboration of some experts and professional collectors of wooden antiques from the nineteenth century. This design combines bookshelves with a bunk bed, a bench, and a corridor, forming the curved shape of a guitar and its strings, which also resemble the curves of a female body."

As Andras traced the visionary shape next to An, she felt an overwhelming desire to hold his hand. But instead, she simply stood there, reminiscing about the moment when she had stepped out of a cab in Ha Noi, and Andras had offered his hand to her. Placing her small hand in his large one, she

had felt an indescribable warmth and a sense of trust, like no other hand had ever given her.

And now, she yearned to draw closer to him, to bury her face in those warm and reassuring hands.

"I want to take a shower," she suddenly declared, merely to prevent herself from getting lost in her thoughts. The tepid water from the shower washed away the fatigue and restraints of the long flight, cleansing her mind so that she could return to her true self, unencumbered by any distractions or temptations that might trouble her soul.

The concert hall came alive with the enchanting strains of a popular piece.

Amateur dancers, brimming with passion for their country's traditional dance, led each other gracefully to the dance floor. An and Andras sat on the wooden stairs among the audience. Mesmerized by the exuberant music and the skillful moves of the male dancers, An found herself wishing she were a man born in Budapest like Andras, who could dance with unbridled ecstasy on his legendary legs.

"Would you like to dance with me?" Andras stood before An, extending his hands to her.

"I can't dance!" An exclaimed, feeling overwhelmed by the complexity of the dance. "It's too tricky; I don't think I can do it."

"Don't worry, I'll lead you. Just follow me," Andras assured her, drawing closer, their cheeks gently touching. His eyes were pleading, and An couldn't resist. She allowed herself to be taken by him, completely besotted.

For the first time in her life, An experienced the exotic dance of the land where the Danube poetically flowed, nurturing generation after generation of fervent young people who danced like flames on their erotic legs.

She surrendered herself to Andras as he swirled her away in the dance. He moved around her with a passionate fire that engulfed her entirely. His feet stomped on the floor like a fierce wind, a storm, a mysterious tempest, turning her into his wind, his endless flows of passion. She let go of all inhibitions and danced with abandon, becoming one with the dance, the embodiment of passion.

In Andras' arms, she lost herself, seeking fulfillment in his embrace, even if only for a fleeting moment. The Budapest night enveloped them, infusing her

with its essence, flowing within her veins. She unleashed her desires to their fullest, yearning to merge with him, even if it was just for a single moment.

Andras held her tight in his whirlwind of passion, his fervent energy coursing through her. They danced as one, body and soul entwined in a passionate embrace.

Leading her to his house, the sweet chill of the late Budapest evening contrasted with the fiery emotions raging within them. He drew her inside, shutting the door behind them.

In his arms, she felt his powerful embrace, and yet, it softened into tenderness. He kissed her, cherishing her more than anything. In that moment, he could have conquered the hearts of countless girls with his desire. But with An, he feared that her purity and the fragile memory of their first meeting at the Poetry Festival in Quán Gió would vanish. She was his muse, a light he would treasure for eternity. He wouldn't harm even a single strand of her hair, the same hair that shimmered like sunlight in Ha Noi.

Nuzzling her head against his chest, An could hear his heartbeat. He closed his eyes, inhaling the fragrance of Ha Noi in her hair, wanting her to linger in his arms forever. His heart ached as she let go, dropping her arms from his body.

"An, hold me a little bit longer, won't you? Don't let go of me!" Andras murmured in silence. Why was it so? He was there, and the girl he desired so intensely that he dared not touch her was now letting him slip away.

An stood there, a mere foot away from him, delicate and radiant in the pure light. She had returned to herself, and the torment within him faded away.

***

Andras and An strolled into Budakeszi Airport on the outskirts of Budapest, where a vast expanse of grass stretched out, waiting for helicopters to take flight. Andras had already arranged for one to soar with her in the skies above Budapest, offering a bird's-eye view of the enchanting city. An was left speechless as Andras settled into the pilot's seat.

"You can fly a helicopter?" she finally asked, curious. "How long have you been flying?"

"This is my first time," Andras smiled playfully, teasing her. "I knew you would come to Budapest and stay with me, so I had to do this impossible thing!"

"Are you kidding me? I'm terrified. I hope you aren't carrying pistols and wearing a bullet-proof vest!" She shook her head, feeling a mixture of panic and excitement. Nonetheless, she followed him into the cockpit and settled beside pilot Andras. Her eyes scrutinized him from head to toe, and in that cockpit, he seemed like a mysterious figure. Was he still the same Andras she thought she knew? No, she realized she hadn't truly known him at all! He winked at her before focusing on starting the engine. The noise rumbled as the helicopter roared to life, and it began to glide along the grassy runway, shaking with vigor. An's heart fluttered with both dread and exhilaration. Would she soar gracefully or plummet helplessly, shattering into pieces? The helicopter lifted off, and she felt a sensation of falling, mirroring the chopper's shaky ascent. She dared not look at Andras.

As they ascended higher, An gazed down at the meandering blue Danube River, flowing like a silk ribbon below. The grand bridges seemed tiny from this perspective. Budapest's panorama looked different and captivating from up here. An's fear vanished, replaced by awe as she marveled at the hills, woods, and rooftops of houses. The ancient palaces atop the hills, the intertwining streets, churches, and castles all appeared like splendid toys sparkling in the sunshine along the river.

The helicopter's blades suddenly dipped, and An felt like she was falling freely. Her heart seemed to drop along with the blades. Terrified, she clutched the handrests of her seat. Just when she thought the chopper would crash into Gellért Hill's ancient place, it swiftly rose and hovered above the hilltop. Andras laughed gleefully, having sought to frighten her to her core. She swore to herself that if she survived this impromptu flight, she would definitely get back at him.

Upon landing, An felt dizzy and disoriented. Even a flight enthusiast like her had been shaken to her core by this daring adventure in the air. Standing next to the helicopter, waiting for Andras to complete the paperwork, she still felt the sensation of flight, dizzy and euphoric. It was the most terrifying yet exhilarating experience she had ever encountered. Despite the beautiful late March weather with its gentle sunshine and refreshing chill, An, a literary wizard, found herself at a loss for words to describe her emotions. All she could call it was a moment of eternity.

Andras returned, touching her shoulders with a smile. He appeared as an enigmatic Andras she thought she knew a little or perhaps not at all. A striking Andras!

"Are you alright?" he asked gently.

"I'm not," she shook her head. "I never knew the person I met was a cunning James Bond of Hungary."

"And what about you? Are you the lady of James Bond or his wife?" Andras squinted, hoping for an answer.

"Nope. I'd be a disaster as James Bond," An retorted, finally awakening from her reverie.

"You're not. You are a dream..." Andras offered his hand, inviting An to intertwine her fingers with his.

They walked together in the soft sunshine and sweet spring breeze of Budapest. The path seemed to stretch on endlessly for these two free spirits who had long shunned the idea of marriage.

CHAPTER TWO
NIGHT BUTTERFLIES IN HA NOI

Walking briskly toward the exit of Hall A at Noi Bai airport, Andras couldn't help but steal a glance at the eager crowd waiting for An. Their eyes locked with his, and in that moment, he felt a rush of warmth and passion. An ran towards him, her face beaming with joy, and they embraced tightly as he planted a loving kiss on her cheek.

"Hi, Hanoi!" Andras greeted her with a smile.

"Hello, Budapest!" An replied, taking his hand and guiding him through the crowd. "Look who else is here to welcome you."

Bang approached, extending his hand to Andras with a smile. "I envy you! Men in this land can never touch An. I've tried many times but never succeeded in hugging her. You're quite the mischief-maker, Andras."

"It's not just hugging and kissing," Andras said playfully, placing an arm around An's shoulder. "We have a partnership in this endeavor, and together we can conquer these hapless men in this country."

"If only you'd break 'the Budapest vow,'" An teased. "The Budapest vow? What's that?" Bang asked, curious.

"When we were in Budapest, we fell in love, but we vowed never to touch each other's bodies, sort of a platonic love," Andras explained.

"Sounds like a joke to me," Bang chuckled. "Love should be genuine, not just a poetic imagination. Your romantic poetry is beautiful, but in real life, that kind of love might not be enough. Anyway, it's Budapest's vow, not Hanoi's. You must love this girl with all your heart and soul, not just in poetry."

***

The book launch of "Enchanting Hanoi" by Andras drew a massive crowd at the National Fine Arts Museum's front yard, despite the drizzling rain. Hungarians living in Vietnam, Vietnamese alumni who studied in Hungary, embassy staff, poets, writers, and many more gathered to witness the event.

Andras's poems about Hanoi had captured the hearts of readers with his unique perspective on the city and his extraordinary love for it. People were eager to see the muse who inspired such beautiful verses. An and Bang co-hosted the launch, presenting a captivating spectacle. An's sharp wit and eloquence added to the allure of Andras's poetry, creating an atmosphere of mystery and intrigue.

After the event, attendees were both satisfied and curious, as Andras remained tight-lipped about his secret lover. He was surrounded by admirers, clamoring for his attention and seeking his autograph. Young women boldly flirted with him, trying to catch his eye and get his contact information. Andras reveled in the attention, feeling ecstatic amid the whirlwind of admiration and interest in his work.

***

"Andras, are you ready?" An exclaimed excitedly. "Today, we have the whole day to explore Hanoi by motorbike, just like the wish I told you back in Budapest."

"He wanted to blend in the mysterious mist of Hanoi," Andras murmured, rubbing his eyes. Was it An? She looked so different in that military outfit and photographer's pocket vest. Her hair was tied up, and she wore a blue-and-white helmet, giving her a mischievous and boyish appearance as she stood next to the dusty motorbike. Andras felt the urge to playfully punch her shoulders, and he even raised his fist...

"Andras!" An dodged, laughing. "Don't be so violent. Today, I'll be your chauffeur. Behave yourself, man!"

"Alright, let me be your chauffeur," Andras agreed.

"But you have no idea about Hanoi traffic. There are no rules here!" An warned.

"The more rules people know, the more accidents they may cause. Less law, more humanity!" Andras replied. "I'll drive the motorbike, and you can drive me."

"Great!" An burst into laughter, allowing Andras to take the lead.

They weaved through the bustling traffic, Andras speeding through yellow lights and braking abruptly at red ones, causing An to collide with his back. An became frustrated and playfully punched his side, to which he chuckled. Throughout the day, Andras kept asking for food and drinks, and An guided him to the most delicious street eateries, making them forget the shabby surroundings as they enjoyed the delightful cuisine. Andras's eyes sparkled with joy as he watched An savor every bite, and he couldn't have asked for a more blissful moment.

"An, I have a stomach ache," Andras suddenly said, pulling over to the roadside, wincing in pain. "Hanoi's food is both delicious and poisonous. Can you show me the way to the Vietnam-France hospital?"

"Oh, no, that hospital is very expensive!" An exclaimed. "You don't need to go there. Let's find a restroom, and you'll be fine."

"You must be killing me, An," Andras frowned. "Let's go to a nearby hotel; I can't hold it any longer."

They spotted a four-star hotel by the roadside, and despite having explored the city all day, they decided to seek refuge in the comfort of the hotel. An rushed outside to find stomach medicine and digestive aids while speaking with the receptionist. But when she returned to the room with the medication, Andras was nowhere to be found.

An asked the hotel staff, who directed her to room 007. With a sense of urgency, she knocked on the door, but there was no response. She pushed the door open, and her heart sank at the sight of Andras lying motionless on the bed, covered with a white sheet. Rushing to his side, she called his name, but he didn't respond. His hand was cold, and he wasn't breathing.

"Andras, please don't frighten me," An whispered, her voice trembling. She hugged him tightly, pressing her ear to his chest to listen for a heartbeat.

Suddenly, Andras sat up and held An tightly, rolling her onto her side and lying beside her on the bed. He gripped her so firmly that it almost hurt. She was torn between happiness and frustration, trying to push him away. Andras entwined his legs and arms with hers, burying his face in her hair, as he whispered in a husky voice, "I want you. I couldn't resist your allure. Break the vow, honey."

"Let me go," An pleaded, her heart conflicted. "Please, return to Budapest."

***

Andras sent An a text to apologize, but her mind was adrift, knowing that he hadn't made any mistake. He had stopped at the edge, just as she had. It was An who wanted to fall into that abyss with him, but she needed to control her desires. She couldn't satisfy those desires herself; they would wither away like countless others in the world. An wanted to stay away from conventional love, with all its entanglements and commitments. She valued her freedom, and she refused to be shackled by any conventional love affair. Andras understood and accepted that. The price they would have to pay for their romantic and ethereal love was to fight against their instinctual desires.

She texted him, saying she would be busy all day, suggesting that he explore Hanoi with another friend to see different angles without her influence. An put on a smart outfit, light makeup, and headed to an appointment as a ghostwriter for a businessman's memoir.

Reading An's text, Andras felt empty. He reached for his tobacco kit, rolled a cigarette, and lit it, trying to clear his mind. He struggled with the duality of love - the need for inspiration for his poetry while restraining his physical desires. He thought of An and the tears welled up in his eyes.

His phone chimed with a message from an unknown number. It was from a bold girl who had flirted with him at his book launch. She had a fascination with him and often asked him for ideas about his poems. He called her, and they agreed to meet at a bar in Hanoi.

In the dimly lit bar, Dung, the girl, seduced him with her appearance, but Andras found no real satisfaction in their encounter. He felt hollow, thinking of An. After their brief encounter, Dung revealed that she knew An, referring to her as the literary wizard with a whimsical image. She insinuated that An might be involved with a wealthy man, using her image to make money. But Andras didn't want to hear any backbiting about An.

Later, Andras found himself outside An's house, unsure whether to approach or leave. He had done a terrible thing and questioned the reality of his experiences in Hanoi. His thoughts were muddled, and he felt lost. Seeing An with another man in a Mercedes added to his torment, and he fled the scene.

On the flight back to Budapest, he called Bang, seeking honesty and advice. Bang reminded him to protect his soul and be cautious of the temptations in this land.

Andras received a message from An but was afraid to read it, fearing that he would either be unable to leave Hanoi or leave forever. As the plane took off, he felt a jolt in his heart, gasping for air. His cellphone fell from his hand, and he realized that his heart was no longer there.

Ha Noi faded from view, and Andras put his hand to his chest, feeling as if his heart had departed with the city.

CHAPTER THREE
THE WOMAN ON THE HILLTOP

Andras arrived home late after a long day of work on the software project with the German customer. The pressure and rigor of his job forced the poet inside him to take a backseat, focusing on the IT expertise needed for the final stages of the project.

As he entered his condo, he was taken aback to find An, the Hanoian girl, standing by his door. Her eyes were filled with tears, and she looked vulnerable and forlorn. All her masks of vanity, the image of a literary wizard, were dropped, and she stood there as a woman in need of comfort and understanding.

Andras remained calm, silently approaching and embracing her, holding her like a father would hold his little daughter. They stood there, seeking solace and warmth in each other's arms. He led her to the couch next to the bookshelf, still keeping his arm around her, not wanting her to vanish like the fleeting fog in Ha Noi.

He gently wiped away her tears and kissed her cheeks and eyes, apologizing for the hurt he had caused by leaving Ha Noi without a word, cutting off all communication. He acknowledged that he had been heartless and wondered if he had done it to torment her or to see her experience the pain he felt.

An found the courage to speak up, asking him to be honest about his feelings. Did he truly love her, or was she merely a role model they had created for each other?

In a tender voice, Andras confessed, "I love you. You are my dream, my purest Muse. You embody the essence of Ha Noi in my eyes. Thank you for coming here and bringing my heart back to me."

An, still shaken by the hurt he had caused, asked him to clarify his feelings, to ensure that it was genuine love and not just an infatuation with the role they had assigned each other. Andras gently stroked her hair as they continued their heartfelt conversation.

"Why don't you and that role model blend into one? Why do you separate yourself from it?" An questioned with a mix of curiosity and pain.

"Because I was broken. That night in Ha Noi, while you felt abandoned, I slept with a stranger," Andras confessed, his hands no longer caressing her hair as he turned away.

"And the next morning, when you saw me with another man in front of your house, did that association lead to your decision? I searched all over Ha Noi for you, and Bang told me you inquired about me. Perhaps your dream was shattered," An poured out her emotions, her face flushed.

"An, please stop. I fear we're falling into the trap of jealousy," Andras said, rising to his feet and gently pulling An's hands. "Come back to our paths. It's dark now, but I want to show you something."

***

On that mid-autumn evening, Budapest was cold yet softly illuminated. Andras swiftly guided An through the Elisabeth Bridge and found a parking spot. Hand in hand, they ascended Gellert Hill alongside the Danube River. The stone steps seemed to stretch on forever, with trees casting mysterious shadows over their path, and soft yellow lights guiding their way.

An's heart raced as she climbed the steep hill. Sensing her struggle, Andras turned back and kneeled down, offering his back as a sturdy support. An was touched by his warm gesture and eagerly embraced him, allowing him to carry her uphill. Her face nestled next to his ears, eyes closed, savoring the moment and inhaling deeply as the night wind caressed her hair and mingled with Andras's warm breath.

"Do you know the legend of Gellert Hill?" Andras inquired playfully.

"I don't," An replied, her face still against his shoulder, her hair cascading down his chest.

According to the legend, every night, witches would climb Gellert Hill. However, they were cunning creatures who preferred not to walk by themselves. Instead, they would sit on someone's back and make them carry them wherever they desired, as they aimed to reach the hilltop using others' feet.

"Andras!" An exclaimed, pounding lightly on his shoulders. "What are you implying? Why did the witches go up there?"

"To read poetry and search for Hungary's James Bond!" Andras chuckled. "Please, let me down. I'll walk up the hill myself," An playfully scolded him, pressing her finger to his forehead. "You've sweated. I don't want to be a witch

anymore. In Ha Noi, I've been called the literary witch for all my life."

Andras gently set An down on the stone steps. "I walk up this hill almost every night, so no problem," he assured her, taking her hands and walking beside her.

He shared a philosophical observation about the chaotic world, where real and surreal elements were intertwined, causing people to lose their souls, with only their shadows remaining.

An looked up at him, seeking further clarity. "So you wanted me to come here just to tell me that I am a witch, and you are a human?"

"I am a human, most of the time," Andras replied with a grin, suddenly hugging her tenderly. "Stay with me, so I can be a human, my lovely witch."

They paused at a protruding balcony near the hilltop, where they could admire the Danube from above. An stood in awe, beholding the magnificent river and the dazzling city adorned with twinkling stars along the banks. The beauty of nature combined with the poetic grandeur of human innovation captivated her. But even more captivating was the man beside her, the Budapest man whom she loved deeply.

Undercurrents surged from the Danube, connecting them, and in that moment, they shared a bond more profound than any words could express.

The deep anguish of their separation and the countless unreturned questions that had haunted An since Andras left Ha Noi were finally starting to heal. She wrapped her arms around him, drawing him close for their first kiss by the Danube River – a pure and sweet moment. An had shed her protective cloak, allowing herself to be vulnerable and open with him.

Sitting atop Gellert Hill, they immersed themselves in the mesmerizing lights that illuminated the sculpture of the lady standing at the summit of Budapest – a symbol of the city's liberty. Andras brought her to a spot where the view of the sculpture was most beautiful.

"Look at the woman on the summit," he said softly. "That's the beacon of freedom, human beauty, and love, all of which reside on the highest peak of Budapest, where I belong."

Andras questioned why there were no female statues in Ha Noi, and An playfully replied that Hanoian women were busy with their lives, fulfilling countless responsibilities. Andras conceded the point and teased An, joking about how her statue would attract unwanted attention from men if it were placed in Ha Noi.

As part of a collaborative literary project between Vietnam and Hungary, Andras introduced An to a popular Hungarian novelist named Istvan at the Szimpla Kertmozi bar. Andras excused himself, leaving An and Istvan to discuss the translation of Istvan's novel, "Destruction," into Vietnamese.

An was captivated by Istvan's charm, finding herself drawn into his enigmatic world. Andras had warned her about Istvan's reputation as a womanizer, and he expressed concern about introducing her to him.

Later, Istvan proposed a collaboration with An, wanting to write a book together in English, seeing her as an exotic muse from the Orient. Tempting as the offer was, An expressed her reservations, citing the language barrier as a concern.

As Istvan approached her with a goblet of red wine, An thanked him but stated that she needed time to think about the proposal before giving a final answer. His cunning smile only deepened her suspicion, and she knew she had to tread carefully in this new territory.

The evening drew on, leaving An with a whirlwind of thoughts and emotions. As she stood there, she realized that her life had taken an unexpected turn. The future was uncertain, and she wondered where this journey would lead her. Yet, she knew that amidst the chaos and unpredictability, the beacon of her love for Andras remained steady and unwavering.

"This," Istvan proclaimed, presenting a glass of wine, "is the most special type of wine in this region, reserved for the most distinguished guest. Please try it and see what happens…"

An hesitated, gazing at the glass. She felt the intense gaze of the man standing beside her, his passion palpable. A part of her wanted to escape, but she didn't want to hurt him either.

Suddenly, Istvan's hands were on her shoulders, drawing her closer. His face loomed near, and An felt her head spin, causing her to drop the wine glass. Reacting instinctively, she raised her knees to keep him at a distance.

But just as things took an unsettling turn, a powerful punch landed on Istvan's face, striking his eyes and disorienting him. It was Andras, who had appeared out of nowhere, his voice laced with fury as he spoke Hungarian to Istvan. He swiftly pulled An away from the scene.

The sedan raced away like an arrow, and Andras sped up towards an intersection. An held on tightly, feeling as if their car might crash and shatter them both into pieces. But suddenly, Andras executed a sharp U-turn at the intersection, causing An to fall onto his side. His anger was unbridled.

At the bottom of the hill, Andras parked the car, and An stepped out, exhaling frosty air. She noticed that one of the car's back wheels was lifted off the ground. Andras paid no mind to it, pulling An towards the woods. The serene cold of the deep forest seemed to calm him.

An leaned her head on his shoulders, asking softly, "It wasn't alright, was

it?"

Andras responded, "It was. The only thing that wasn't alright was a plot."

"But you already punched him. What if he cancels everything we agreed on earlier?" An worried.

"Those are two different things. Here, men resort to violence when words fail. The punch was to awaken his sense of morality," Andras explained, lifting An's face to look deeply into her eyes. "I believe the agreements will still hold, and he will come to understand where to draw the line. Sometimes, we have no choice but to believe in humanity."

An heard the words, "Believe in humanity," as the breeze from the Western woods carried them away into the air, harmonizing with the whispers of the canopy above. In that moment, she found comfort and reassurance in the presence of her beloved.

CHAPTER FOUR
TRAVEL IN MEMORY

Andras gently turned the doorknob, eager to surprise An. He imagined she might be engrossed in a book or absorbed in writing a new romantic short story on her laptop. He planned to sneak up behind her, holding his breath, and softly kiss her delicate earlobe, hoping her long hair would be pulled back to reveal her small ears.

However, as he tiptoed into the common room, Andras found no sign of An reading on the cozy sofa, covered with a soft, burgundy geometric throw. He noticed a slight crease in the fabric, suggesting she had recently occupied the spot.

Curiosity led Andras to glance toward the balcony, where a flimsy white curtain swayed like a thin veil of mist. Pulling the curtain aside, he discovered An leaning on the balcony railing, her eyes fixed on the view of Freedom Bridge across the Danube. The picturesque scene cast a golden glow over the century-old buildings, reminiscent of a bygone era captured in a black-and-white movie.

Unaware of Andras's return, An wept silently, her gaze tracing the end of the street where the sunset wove a vibrant yellow thread over the bridge.

Concerned, Andras approached her, placing his hands gently on her shoulders and turning her towards him. "An, what's wrong? I'm back. Come on, honey," he whispered tenderly.

An buried her face in Andras's shoulders, trying to stifle her runny nose as she spoke, "I'm sorry... Not because of you, but because my aunt just passed away in Vietnam."

Andras reached into his pocket, offering her a handkerchief to wipe away her tears. With a gentle smile, he assured her, "You look beautiful when you cry. But you don't have to lure me with your tears. Your smile is enough to melt my

heart. But tell me, why do you cry over your aunt's passing? Did you feel guilty for something when she was alive?"

"No, not at all!" An looked up at him, her eyes still teary. "Where did you get that idea? How could you even joke about death?"

Andras chuckled softly, trying to bring some levity to the somber moment. "I suppose it's just my way of accepting the natural cycle of life. Everyone will face the end eventually, including me. If I were to pass away, would you cry like this for me too?"

An's heart swelled with emotion, and she chided him, "Andras, don't talk like that! You're not going anywhere anytime soon."

Their tender exchange brought them closer, reminding them of the preciousness of their time together. As Andras comforted An, he realized that life's journey was filled with both joy and sorrow, and they were fortunate to have each other to lean on in times of need. The beauty of the moment was magnified by the golden hues of the setting sun, casting a warm glow over their embrace.

In the silence of that tranquil evening, Andras and An discovered that even amidst loss and heartache, their love remained a beacon of light, guiding them through the vast expanse of memories and emotions.

"Then you will definitely cry when I die. Don't treat me like that. Please stroke my eyes to close, and play the song 'La Vie en Rose.' While I'm alive, love me with all your heart, with all of you, then when I depart this life, you won't have to cry."

An embraced him tightly, tears welling up in her eyes, yet her heart strangely calm. She loved this man, deeply and passionately. Gratitude swelled within her for the fate that brought him to her—the man who saw her true self, empowering her in ways she had never imagined. On the balcony of the fourth floor of this ancient building, a gentle breeze carried with it a splendid golden sunset, wrapping the young couple in an embrace akin to the amorous artwork of sculptor Benjamin Shine. The allure of the sunset spread its radiance through the streets and adorned the top of Freedom Bridge with a golden crown. An cherished this sunset, always ablaze with a pure, intense, and glorious glow

before gracefully fading away. Here, in one of the most enchanting quarters of Budapest, she found herself wrapped in the arms of this beautiful man, whose poet's mind traversed time and space, unbound by convention. Was this a dream? Even in his embrace, she yearned for him profoundly, knowing that she would eventually leave him, bound by her unyielding vow of a celibate life. A love unconstrained, a love that knew no marriage, only an unending journey in memory. A love that remembered and yearned incessantly—a desire that would never find satiation.

The night before An's departure to Prague, where she would negotiate a book contract with an overseas Vietnamese merchant, Andras took her to Ladó Café on Dohány Street—a romantic bar known for its live music, featuring favorite Jazz bands of Budapest residents.

Reserving a private table for two, they enjoyed a lovely view near the small stage where the band played romantic and improvised Jazz songs. An's smile illuminated her face as she noticed a crystal vase of red roses, leaning slightly, catching the flickering candlelight and adorning their table, complete with a nameplate. Andras assisted her in taking off her coat, draping it carefully on a rack behind their seats. From across the table, he gazed at her silently, exuding a graceful aura. The soft golden light played upon her face, accentuating her dark, tucked-back hair cascading gently to her chest. Her dark cobalt blue wool dress, with its faint red stripes, draped her shoulders charmingly, enticing him to reach out and feel her warmth. Oh, how he missed her, even though she sat merely an arm's length away, knowing that come tomorrow morning, she would be gone again. He tried to conceal a sigh, not wanting to dampen the evening.

Andras understood her as a freelance writer, a true digital nomad, exploring and writing about the world she traversed. It was her passion, and he knew he could never hinder it. No matter how much of himself or his world he offered, she would not crash-land in his arms. He, Budapest, and their memories and love would remain, while she ventured forth, leaving behind an endless yearning.

Since she had dared to break free from the shackles of a thousand years of enduring customs imposed on women in her homeland, how could he possibly keep her confined in this liberating Europe?

As the waiter arrived, bearing a bottle of her favorite white wine, she savored its flavor with ecstasy, nodding her approval. The effervescent wine frothed around the glass's thin rim, and Andras gazed at her passionately with a beguiling smile. The waiter poured wine for both of them, placing the bottle in an ice bucket while wishing them a delightful dinner. An averted her eyes, fearing she might lose herself in Andras's endearing gaze, causing her to reconsider and stay forever in this place, amidst a Budapest romance akin to a fairy tale, with the man she loved more than life itself.

Born in Vietnam, a country where most women were expected to marry, considering it the greatest blessing, she had chosen a different path. Instead, she embraced a life of independence, desiring to travel and write—

an adventurous existence, one that many could not even dare to dream. She treasured the fate that brought Andras into her life, for he ignited an eternal flame within her, inspiring the younger generation in her homeland to embrace a life as full and free as hers, to shatter conventions and prejudices, and to conquer the impossible.

As waiters brought them a fragrant traditional fish soup, accompanied by chili and onions, served with bread that delighted their taste buds with its sweetness, An found herself already full, declining the dessert of three-colored ice cream. Andras's eyes sparkled with delight as the ice cream was presented.

He regretted that she could no longer enjoy it. She, in turn, admired him in his carefully chosen white shirt for the solemn occasion, making him as enchanting and jubilant as a groom in a peculiar wedding ceremony.

The band from France began to play bohemian and seductive swings. Suddenly, a female singer in a mysterious black dress took the stage and sang "La Vie en Rose." Instantly, Andras stopped eating his ice cream, blurting out, "An old song. A worn romance."

"An old melody, I know, but I still want you to tell me, I still want to hear it with you," An whispered, filled with joy.

Andras, why are you so sweet to me? Why don't you lock me up in your house so I can't go anywhere? What's wrong with me? Do I still resent being tied down?

An was overwhelmed by her own thoughts, and tears suddenly welled up. She wasn't sure if it was the song's impact or the enchanting atmosphere of the place. All she knew was that she had to flee, to run away from this intense desire, a fantasy that threatened to consume her.

At a red light, she paused at the crosswalk, and in that moment, Andras caught up to her.

"An, are you playing the runaway bride? Not a chance, because I'll run with you. Let's sprint—we haven't paid, and the owner is chasing us!" Andras laughed as they took off together.

Andras draped the forgotten coat over An's shoulders and took her hand, urging her to run swiftly along the sidewalk. A few passersby glanced at them in surprise, witnessing this unexpected display of haste.

***

An awoke to a silent house, listening intently. Perhaps Andras was still sleeping, or maybe he sat thoughtfully in front of the computer. She slipped out of bed, opened the bedroom door, and tiptoed into the living room. There, Andras slept on a bunk bed with a railing and a tall bookshelf that reached the ceiling. He had a fondness for sleeping on a bunk bed, reminiscent of his childhood days, just as An recalled her own time dreaming endless children's dreams while resting on similar bunks.

"Hello, Andras," she whispered, her voice soft and gentle.

He stirred from his elevated slumber, looking down at her with eyes full of warmth. "Did you sleep well?" he asked.

"Very well, perhaps it was the white wine we drank last night," she replied.

"I slept well too, feeling refreshed. I hardly ever wake up this late," Andras said, glancing at the clock. "It's already past seven o'clock. Let's have breakfast at a restaurant on the way to the Népliget bus station. It takes just about ten minutes to drive from here. The bus leaves at 9:30 AM, so we can set off at 8:30 AM."

Andras climbed down the ladder from the high bed, holding onto the skillfully curved handrail attached to the wooden structure. As he turned around, An greeted him with a customary morning hug. He cherished these tender embraces from her, a new source of energy to embark on each day's journey.

"Why did you avoid my hug last night?" Andras playfully inquired, mischief in his eyes.

"I drank a lot of wine, and you seemed thirsty. I saw a flicker in your eyes, and I was afraid of getting burned if I touched you," An explained with a smile.

Andras laughed. "You're quite something. You know that I dare not touch the deepest parts of you. Anyway, as you're heading to Prague, beware of the free sex movement spreading across Europe. Don't get entangled in it."

An was curious. "What is it all about?"

"The young people are demanding more freedom in the right to enjoy sex. They've gone mad with their demands, listing more than twenty different types of sex that must be recognized by law, including the right to have sex with animals and even the dead. It's unbelievable," Andras replied.

An shook her head in disbelief. "Don't they have anything better to do? There are so many urgent problems in the world, like plastic waste pollution. How can they be preoccupied with such absurdities?"

Andras grinned. "Well, what about us? Love without sex, isn't that unusual? Isn't it considered a kind of sickness? Perhaps we should start a movement advocating for nonsexual love. But I fear the world might mock me or label me as impotent."

An laughed. "Or they might see me as a dangerous person if I started a movement where women don't engage in relationships, marry, or have children. Probably more dangerous than wars."

"And maybe some men would like that, having more free women on the streets," Andras teased. "They could approach any woman they desire without the fear of being punched by another man. Men have been strong since ancient times, and how they choose to engage in sex is up to them. After all, there must be sex for children to be born and inherit the earth."

Ann playfully retorted, "You still think like a Kitchen God. Have you ever seen one in my country? There's a legend about a Kitchen God who had no wife, no sex, yet his life remained fruitful and abundant."

"Enough of talking about sex so early in the morning. Let's change the subject," Andras declared resolutely, taking a step toward her. "How about discussing the poem you wrote yesterday, or your short story, or even jazz?"

"Those are all banal topics," An said, shaking her head. "Let's go back to talking about sex."

"Fine, but on the condition that you write down the name of the jazz band that played at Ladó Cafe last night. I want to find more of their songs online," An said, digressing.

Andras smirked, pulling her hand toward his computer. He turned on the phone and searched for the band's name. Suddenly, An exclaimed as she glanced at the lower right corner of the computer screen—it showed 9:30 AM.

"Andras, look! Why does it say 9:15?"

"It can't be," Andras stared at the screen, then back at the clock on the wall, which read 8:15.

"Oh my God," Andras put his hand over his head, realizing the mistake. "I forgot to set the clock on the wall. Today is the last Sunday in March, Europe- wide daylight-saving time, one hour ahead of wintertime. We have to hurry to the bus station if you don't want to miss your bus to Prague."

An swiftly changed her clothes as Andras carried her suitcase. They ran! "It only takes six minutes to drive from my house to the bus station. I've

set a new record," Andras said while carrying An's suitcase, sprinting towards

the laurel green bus bound for Prague. It was the bus An had booked in advance for her journey. "You go show your passport to the conductor, I'll go to the convenience store to get you some breakfast."

An gasped for breath as she was the last to board the bus. Andras handed her a brown bag, hugged and kissed her quickly on the cheek. She found a seat, and as the bus pulled away, she looked out the window. There stood Andras on the sidewalk of the bus station, placing his hand over his heart and bowing like an artist. He danced, performing the traditional male dance with the legendary legs of the blue Danube country—the land of love and passionate, passionate dance. He danced for her, and tears welled up in her eyes. She wanted to rush back to him, but the bus continued on, leaving behind an ardent heart dancing in a fiery spectacle, fading into the distance as she wept.

"I'm just a journey Meeting, then parting

Deep in the heart of Danube You look up to find me

The woman on top of the mountain

The angel so far away, with a broken heart..."

Andras's poetic lines from the previous night echoed in her mind as An hunched over, tormented by emotions. Andras, don't you know that you are the place I want to come and stay, in the endless journey of my life.

CHAPTER FIVE
THE DICHOTOMY OF LOVE

Restless on the weekend, Andras paced his apartment on the fourth floor of an old building on Bartók Béla Street. The vastness of the space and the multitude of books adorning gleaming wooden shelves seemed to offer no solace, leaving him feeling empty and lost. His eyes fell upon a light blue paperback, An's collection of short stories titled "Virtual Wife." Though beautifully written in Vietnamese, it remained indecipherable to him. He gently returned the book to its place.

Moving to the kitchen table, his gaze fixed on a small red tea box adorned with an image of an Asian boy dressed in traditional Vietnamese garb. An had mentioned it was a gift from a Vietnamese engagement ceremony. Andras opened the box, finding only a pinch of dry tea remaining—enough to make a teapot. Had An left it intentionally?

Before her departure from Budapest to Prague, she had prepared a pot of tea, placing a pinch of tea leaves in the flat, delicate teapot, making it challenging for him to clean afterward. For such an antique teapot, using a tea bag would have made the process much easier. An had forgotten to use one, and her little oversight brought a smile to Andras' face. She truly knew how to drive him crazy, playfully calling herself the disaster of his life.

He had once likened her to a dream, but perhaps she was a disaster too. In this moment of restlessness, within the confines of his home—the space he owned and where he could have indulged in leisurely activities like sipping herbal tea, enjoying books, writing love poems, or crafting essays on the waning European values—he found himself drawn back to the world of technology he delved into for five days a week at his office. Weekends, he had always reserved for poetry, music, or movies, freeing himself from the shackles of technology.

He considered himself fortunate for not being entangled in a marriage with children or societal pressures, like other ordinary men. However, since An entered his life like a flame, only to turn into a distant stranger at times, he grappled with acute nostalgia that plagued him. He tried to forget the haunting memories that filled his mind. In a moment of contemplation, he opened his smartphone and accessed the WhatsApp application, delving into the extensive conversations between him and An.

His eyes brightened as a thought crossed his mind. He had once discovered a security flaw in this application. As a skilled information technology expert, he often amused himself by exploring errors in popular technology products within the IT industry, either for fun or professional development. This time, he decided to utilize the flaw for a different purpose.

Andras' face flushed red as he considered the implications. Could a master hacker for a prominent Hungarian information technology company allow himself to act as a hacker? He sighed, realizing that nothing was impossible. He refrained from making excuses, acknowledging the moral complexity of his actions.

***

The massive FX bus slowly rolled to a halt at stop 18 of Florence bus station, located south of Prague. The driver, dressed in a uniform that mirrored the vehicle's color, stepped down. Short and agile, with mischievous eyes and an open countenance, he bore no resemblance to a typical Central European. As An approached, she switched on her phone to retrieve the ticket code she had pre- ordered and handed it to him, allowing him to verify it with his handheld ticket machine. His curious gaze made her uneasy, perhaps due to her being the sole Asian passenger on this trans-European bus. Nevertheless, he nodded in confirmation, and she acknowledged his gesture with a slight nod of her own.

"Is this your only piece of luggage?" the driver inquired, pointing to the large black suitcase beside her. An confirmed with a nod, and he promptly stowed it in the compartment below. Grateful, she reached for her phone, capturing a picture of the bus's number plate to send to Andras via WhatsApp. He would need it to identify her when they met at Kelenfold station in Budapest. Settling into her seat by the window, An relished her customary spot that granted a view of the roadside scenery. The eight-hour journey from Prague to Budapest could have been tedious for some, but she found joy in observing the vast farms, forests, green fields sloping up hills with grazing animals, and the charming villages perched halfway up the slopes. The journey ignited her creativity, prompting smiles and inspiring numerous ideas that she diligently noted in her trusty notebook.

After 47 days of work and exploration in Prague and its surroundings, An secured a contract to write a memoir for an overseas Vietnamese businessman residing in the Czech capital. With the deposit already transferred to her account, she felt reassured about the task ahead. The man's chaotic and intriguing life in a foreign land offered fertile ground for her fictionalization. The tight timeframe, however, demanded that she rearrange her burgeoning ideas. This return to

Budapest would extend beyond the usual visits, allowing her to focus on writing while delving deeper into the city's life and culture—a fairy-tale place that made her heart flutter. But was it solely because of Budapest's magnificence, or was it the presence of a certain guy living there?

During the pit stop at Bruno gas station, the junction city in the Czech Republic, passengers took advantage of the ten-minute break to visit the convenience store, grab food, water, or use the restroom. An, too, alighted from the bus, donning a warm coat, and headed to the restroom before leisurely stepping outside to enjoy the scenery. The cluster of daffodils in full bloom caught her attention, signaling the impending arrival of Easter. As she took photographs of the adorable flowers, her gaze wandered to a pine forest nearby, still vibrant amidst the cold season. Hidden within the forest was a rose bud sculpture that piqued her curiosity.

"Hello, teacher!" a slightly squeaky male voice called out.

An turned to find the mischievous-eyed long-distance driver addressing her. "Aren't you buying anything in there?" he asked.

"Well, I brought my own food and drink on the bus, so I didn't need to buy anything else," she responded.

"Are you Chinese?" he asked, curiosity evident in his tone.

"I am Vietnamese," An replied with a smile. "Yellow skin and black hair don't always mean Chinese."

""I apologize, it's just that there are so many Chinese travelers in Europe these days, it seems like every time I open my eyes, I see them talking loudly as if they're arguing," the driver explained with a shrug. "Are you traveling alone?"

An didn't answer immediately; instead, she replied with a question of her own, "What makes it more interesting for you if I'm with other people?"

"Well, I assume that Asian women rarely travel long-distance alone. They usually go in groups and chat. If you need any help, don't hesitate to ask," the driver offered kindly.

"Then how many more stops until Kelenfold?" An inquired.

"We'll stop in Bratislava first, then cross the Bratislava station before heading to the Kelenfold terminus," the driver replied, checking his watch. "We should get back on the bus."

Curious, An asked as she accompanied the driver to the parking spot, "I assume you're not Czech?"

"I'm Colombian. You have a keen eye," the driver winked. "I've been living in the Czech Republic for fifteen years. I drive across Europe and know many border policemen. If you ever have any problems with the police, you can call me. My name is Ramiro. Here's my business card."

An accepted the card but didn't say anything, looking at the name printed on it for a moment.

"Who knows what might happen. I've crossed borders a thousand times, so I know," Ramiro added.

Quietly, An returned to her seat on the bus. Ramiro didn't know her true identity, and she preferred to keep it that way. As a global citizen and a renowned writer, she was well-known in certain circles, but she relished her privacy and the freedom it offered her. Her writing and literary influence were not just personal achievements; they represented a profound connection to her country and all of humanity.

***

The bus made a stop in Bratislava, and several passengers disembarked. An chose to stay away from the crowd, standing on the sidewalk opposite the bus stop, stretching to ease the stiffness from the long journey.

As the time for departure approached, An returned to the bus. However, she froze when she saw three armed policemen blocking the passengers from entering the bus. A search was underway, and some passengers were still waiting beside the vehicle, confused by the situation. An hesitated, unsure whether to get back on the bus or observe from a distance.

Eventually, she decided to board the bus and took her seat, placing her small backpack on her shoulder. However, before she could settle in, a policeman approached her and held up an ID card.

"Hello. I'm a Slovak policeman," the officer stated, his cold blue eyes seeming to pierce into her thoughts. "Please show me your papers."

An opened her backpack, retrieved her passport, and handed it to the towering policeman. She was about to ask why they needed to check her passport but decided against it. In this context, the police had the authority to inquire, not her.

The officer scrutinized her passport carefully before finally returning it. However, the ordeal was far from over. He requested her to step off the bus to confirm her luggage due to a suspicion of illegal baggage.

An complied, alighting from the bus and witnessing what appeared to be an unusual event unfolding before her eyes. The towering policeman then pointed to a black suitcase and asked, "Is this yours?"

"No," An firmly replied, her voice resolute. "That's not my suitcase. My suitcase is also black, but it's Bandicot, and it has a tag with my name and address on it, not this one."

The policeman continued, "All the suitcases in the bus have been pulled down here. Everyone has received their luggage. Only this suitcase is left unclaimed. So where's your suitcase?"

An felt indecisive, aware of the gazes fixed on her from the crowd. She kept her composure, determined to find her suitcase. She searched around, but it was nowhere to be seen. Panic set in; her heart raced. She crouched down, peering into the belly of the bus, but it was empty.

Approaching the tallest policeman, she stammered, "I can't find my suitcase." Her voice trembled, and her mind raced with worry. In that suitcase lay her computer, portable hard drive, and all her belongings. Most importantly, it contained her work - countless documents, manuscripts, and unfinished novels. They were irreplaceable... invaluable.

The policeman pointed to the lone suitcase on the sidewalk, urging her to take a closer look. An obliged but continued to deny its ownership. Doubtful eyes turned to her, and she began to tremble under the pressure.

"If you claim it's not yours, who can testify?" the policeman inquired.

An quickly responded, "The driver. He was the one who lifted my suitcase and put it in the storage compartment at the Florence bus station. He knows my suitcase."

The policeman called the driver over, and he confirmed that the black suitcase belonged to An. Stunned and shaken, she felt her legs weaken beneath her. It seemed that even the person who promised to help her now identified her as the owner of the suspicious suitcase.

"Please follow us with this suitcase," the policeman coldly demanded, his eyes unyielding.

As An complied, she continued to assert that the suitcase wasn't hers. She maintained her composure, relying on her identity as a writer and her accomplishments. She showed the policeman her newly published book, demonstrating that she was a public figure with a reputation to uphold.

"I'm a writer," she declared with confidence, meeting the policeman's gaze firmly. "This is my book. If you search my name on Google, you'll find plenty of information about my activities and works. I would never jeopardize my reputation for anything..."

The policeman acknowledged her status but reminded her that everything was still subject to the law. An called Andras for help, and he assured her that he would provide evidence to prove her innocence. Anxiously, she waited for the promised evidence.

Five minutes felt like an eternity. An's heart raced with uncertainty. Could Andras really pull through in such a short time? She found herself unable to fathom the possibilities, her writer's imagination faltering.

At last, the officer received the evidence from Andras. Relieved, An thanked him. This unexpected ordeal had now become a source of inspiration for her writing. As a writer, she saw even the most challenging moments in life as opportunities to create, to delve into her own experiences fearlessly and courageously. In any situation, life bloomed, and she embraced it, audaciously and amazingly. This incident, too, would be captured in her words, adding another layer of depth to her craft.

After about half an hour, during which An thought the policeman was engrossed in playing games on his smartphone, he finally looked up and spoke. "We have determined this suitcase is not yours. The information from your relatives matches the information we received from a colleague in Prague, where you boarded the bus. You can go. We sincerely apologize for this incident. We will also find your suitcase and return it to you as soon as possible."

Relieved and grateful, An stood up, leaving her business card and Andras' address in Budapest for the police to contact and return her belongings.

However, before leaving, she felt the need to bring something important to their attention.

"Please pay more attention to the driver," she urged. "He seemed to intentionally give false information when he said the suitcase was mine. He knew my suitcase was larger than that. He also boasted about knowing many border policemen and offering to help me if I ever got into trouble, yet he did the opposite."

The policeman reassured her, saying, "Don't worry, we've taken good care of him. Can I offer you a cup of coffee outside the shop near the bus station while you wait for your loved one to pick you up?"

***

Back at Andras' house, An sank into the soft sofa beneath the familiar bunk bed and bookshelf. She was exhausted from the day's events. Andras brought her a glass of mineral water, and she gratefully drank it.

"I don't understand what was in that suitcase, but it felt like they deliberately forced it on me. Was it a terrorist bomb?" An looked at Andras, seeking answers.

Andras shook his head, "Not bombs, but more likely hundreds of millions of dollars or a stash of drugs. Criminals set up a scenario to exchange suitcases. They took your suitcase out of the bus and replaced it with another one. The actual criminal transports the bus, and if everything goes smoothly, he retrieves the suitcase. But if the police intervene, they'll find your suitcase instead. It's a cunning scheme."

An was intrigued but tired, and she asked, "Tell me, Andras, how can I provide them with proof of my suitcase?"

"It's a secret," Andras admitted, feeling embarrassed. "You know I'm like Hungary's James Bond."

"I appreciate that you saved me," An replied wearily, "but I still need to know the truth."

Andras hesitated for a moment before revealing, "Okay, if you insist on knowing. You see, through a vulnerability in the WhatsApp application, I installed a sort of 'bodyguard' in there whose job is to protect you when you're not with me."

"Wait, what?" An was taken aback. "You installed spyware on my phone?

Are you following me? How could you do this to me?"

"I just want to protect you," Andras defended himself. "Now that you're with me, I'll delete it."

An felt speechless and stormed out of Andras' house. He followed her into the hallway, trying to explain himself.

"An, before you leave, you need to hear one last thing from me," Andras pleaded.

An, still upset, turned to him, demanding, "Say it, then."

"If you leave, I will never write poetry again," Andras declared, his voice filled with emotion.

"That's your business, and I don't care," An retorted, ready to walk away. "But wait," Andras spoke louder, determined to make his point. "I'll

switch to writing short fiction instead."

An remained unswayed, replying dismissively, "None of my business."

"On the contrary, it's directly related to you," Andras persisted. "I'll center the stories around you - as both the protagonist and antagonist - so that all men in the world will turn away from you."

An couldn't help but laugh at his dramatic statement. Before she could react further, Andras rushed over and pulled her into a tight embrace, locking her in a passionate kiss.

CHAPTER SIX
AN ORGANIC MARRIAGE

Andras drove away from the bustling center of Budapest, gently swaying to the soulful voice of Louis Armstrong singing "My mama done told me... a woman has a two-face," a smile playing on his lips. An glanced at him, suspicious of his sudden amusement.

"Why do you smile?" she inquired.

"Women have two faces. Especially when they whisper sweetly to me.

As soon as they get what they desire, they leave me lamenting alone in the dark..." Andras took a quick glance at An and then focused on the road ahead. "Are all women like that?"

An remained silent, deciding to change the song to a piece by Fitzgerald. "That song was lovely. Why did you switch to this one? Will Fitzgerald

have a different answer? How many faces do women have?" Andras teased, pretending to raise his voice.

"It depends on her eyes," An replied, tilting her head. "Andras, come with me to Angkor Wat. I'll show you; the Bayon even has four faces!"

"I was just kidding. I'll definitely go to Angkor Wat with you or anywhere you want to go - Mars or Venus, count me in," Andras said with a playful tone, making a sharp turn that caused An to fall lightly against him. She laughed and playfully punched his shoulder.

"Actually, every woman is an angel. Today, I'll show you an angel in the suburbs of Budapest. She's Bella, my friend's wife. They are a typical family. In over eight years of marriage, Bella has given birth to five children, a boy and four girls, and the miracle is that she gave birth to all of them at home, with the help of her husband, without having to visit any hospital or doctor's clinic. All five children are healthy, and my God, they are angels too. You should see them; they are super adorable!" Andras exclaimed.

An looked at him thoughtfully, "Andras, you seem to be enticed by the ordinary married life, aren't you? Are you considering getting married, having children, and...?"

"Me? I'm still unsure of what the future holds for me. But you know, so far, I'm not an ordinary man. I don't necessarily need to have a wife, kids, a stable job, a house, or even an automobile..." Andras replied thoughtfully.

"Is there a particular reason behind this unconventional outlook?" An asked curiously.

"It's just who I am. There's no haunting past or anything like that. Ever since I became aware of myself, I've lived passionately, fully embracing every minute of life. I stay true to myself, whether awake, asleep, or when I'm with you. I am truly a free man," Andras explained with a laugh. "That's the only reason. This lifestyle may seem mundane to others, but I don't concern myself with others' beliefs or societal norms. It doesn't affect me."

An pondered for a moment before asking, "If I decide to get married and we no longer meet or love each other, will it affect you?"

Andras looked at her, his eyes filled with sincerity, "If that's what you choose, I'll respect it. I'll always cherish the moments we shared, even if our paths diverge."

"Do you want to kill me, An?" Andras suddenly accelerated, causing the car to speed up, and An's head and shoulders jerked sharply backward. "I will plunge this car into the Danube, or I will fly a helicopter and crash into the top of Géllert Hill, so the whole world would know and condemn you!"

"Andras, if you want to plunge into the Danube, do it alone. I can't swim, and I'm deadly scared of drowning. But if you want to fly a helicopter over Budapest, take me with you, and then you can take us wherever you want!" An laughed excitedly as Andras geared up, and the wheels spun at the bend of the road.

"Why is there such a demon girl on earth!" Andras thought, smiling.

***

Andras drove down a side street and spotted a magnolia tree in full bloom. He pulled the car over about twenty meters from the magnolia's roots and stepped out, opening the door to help An out. Taking her hand, he led her to a wooden chair under the magnolia tree. In this moment of comfort and light, Andras craved a pipe of fragrant tobacco.

While Andras leisurely puffed his pipe, An wandered around the magnolia tree, counting the branches laden with buds. She knew well that

whenever Andras pulled out his pipe, he would spend at least half an hour intoxicated with the fragrant smoke from that ancient pipe. It was a pleasure she observed in men, a moment of indulgence and reflection. As for herself, her greatest joy came from the rush of ideas and the creation of short stories that would later find their way into prestigious literary newspapers.

"An, sit down with me," Andras called to her, rearranging his smoking kit and stowing it back into a leather bag specially made for pipe smokers. "Now it's your turn to tell me, what makes you want to be single?"

"I want to be a woman who traverses the world, writing ardently day and night, soaring through the skies to the last coin, engaging in endless conversations with you as we sculpt immortal words, mingling with great minds around the world, and discovering the depths of their thoughts," An replied.

"I imagined you had some haunting memories," Andras tilted his head to look at An, "but looking at your pristine appearance, that doesn't seem right. It's only when I peer into your mysterious inner self, your devilish personality, that I think differently..."

"Actually, yes, there are hidden memories not just from myself but from my mother, from aunts in the family, and perhaps even from previous generations of women in the clan," An mused. "Many of them lost themselves after marriage, disappearing into the shadows of their husbands, sons, and daughters. I am different; I don't want to fade away like that. I want to live life on my terms."

"But that can be a blissful existence," Andras gently stroked An's hair, "while you're living a daring and insecure life. Marriage is one of the greatest inventions of human evolution, allowing people to progress a step higher in the journey of learning to be human and live together. Why not fight for a progressive marriage instead of an escape?"

"Because I'm too wise?" An giggled. "Why should I fight, when I'm not certain if I would become a hero or lose my life in the process? I feel sorry for women who struggle with post-marital death, but I choose to leave. The best strategy, among the 36 strategies, is escape for me. I save myself first, and if my actions inspire others to break free from their confinements, it's a welcome bonus. Besides, marriage has already been explored by countless women; my calling is to Go and Write."

"Such a spectacular sight, the magnolia about to bloom, and I'm here with a glamorous lady, talking about evolution and fighting," Andras said with a sly grin. "I must sound like a fool."

An turned to look at Andras, his blue eyes glinting mischievously behind his glasses. She got up and playfully ran away, but Andras was faster. He caught her and held her in his arms, turning her around. An exclaimed, "Andras, take me to your friend's place. Let me see if his organic wife even exists."

"Okay, I'll take you there, if you'll kiss me under this blooming magnolia tree. I want to remember this immortal moment here... I promise to keep it a secret," Andras whispered.

***

Benedek's house nestled at the foot of the pine-covered hill, embraced by a bountiful garden teeming with fruits, vegetables, and a charming fence crafted from uneven pine branches. Both Benedek and his wife, Bella, were ardent advocates of organic living. They baked their own bread and relished vegetables freshly plucked from their garden. On sunny days, their children strolled to school independently, while snowy days witnessed the couple ferrying their little ones by bicycle. Gifts for friends and family came straight from their hands, meticulously fashioned with organic materials sourced from their bountiful garden: paintings adorned with dried leaves and flowers, extraordinary cards made from tree bark, and handwoven wicker baskets. Their creative minds seemed boundless, as they skillfully utilized the abundance provided by the garden in the midst of the pine forest hill.

An stood in awe of Bella's garden, a woman who collected wisdom and toiled diligently until dusk, lovingly tending to every tree and blade of grass.

Each flower and blade of grass seemed to radiate a vibrant cheerfulness under her care. Bella's skillful arrangements lent the garden a resplendent charm. An couldn't help but wonder how Bella managed to care for five children and nurture this enchanting haven all by herself. Surely, she was a superwoman, far from ordinary.

Sadly, Bella was not at home; only Benedek was present, dutifully looking after their five children. Benedek proudly shared that he had recently built a new kitchen with his own hands, entirely fashioned with natural materials. Even the house itself, constructed over eight years ago, was the joint creation of Benedek and Bella, with Bella giving birth to their first child in a bedroom within the walls of an unfinished house.

"Why didn't you inform us about the completion of the new kitchen, so we could bring gifts to celebrate?" Andras inquired.

"We don't need anything from the modern world out there," Benedek insisted. "You can create gifts for us right here, right now."

"How?" Andras asked.

"That white wall there is too bare," Benedek gestured towards the left side of the kitchen. "Bella and I have been pondering whether to hang a picture on it or leave it as it is. But now that you're here, I had a thought—why don't you inscribe a poem on it for us?"

"Well, I carry a plethora of poems wherever I go," said poet Andras, squinting in contemplation.

Venya, Benedek's seven-year-old eldest son, swiftly brought Andras a black fountain pen. Andras propped up a chair, stood with one foot on the chair and the other on the kitchen counter, and began copying poetry on the wall. Once he had finished inscribing his four-line stanza in Hungarian, and stepped down to the kitchen floor, Benedek's second daughter, Aniska, aged six, climbed onto the counter. With the pen Andras had just dropped, she attentively worked on illustrating the poetic lines on the wall.

"What does that line mean?" An asked Andras quietly. She didn't speak Hungarian and only conversed with Andras in English. Fortunately, both of them were passionate about this second language.

"Behind the man is the woman. Behind the woman is silence. Behind the silence, is the void. And behind the void, is a vast mystery..." Andras translated the line of poetry for An.

"Why 'silence'? Why 'mystery'?" An continued to inquire. "Why is the banana curved?" Andras chuckled mischievously.

"I have this dish to reciprocate the poet," Benedek presented a sealed jar of cherries. "My wife made this herself. The dish is unanimously voted by the whole family as the best delicacy in the world."

"Can I eat with you, papa?" The youngest girl, two years old, with bright blue eyes and cheeks as red as ripe apples, ran up to her father, chirping.

Andras and Benedek engaged in an animated conversation in Hungarian, leaving An with the five Benedek children. Though she didn't understand the language, she happily played with them. Venya, the eldest, proved to be hospitable and remarkably mature for his age. He invited An to enjoy a homemade apple pie and brewed tea for her. Venya had a decent grasp of English, allowing them to communicate with ease.

They started by putting two tablespoons on their eyes to make makeshift glasses, capturing pictures together, and laughing heartily. Then, An entertained the children with a peacock dance, and in return, Venya taught her the traditional Hungarian style. An was astonished by the young boy's skillful dancing. The family's spiritual life was truly remarkable. Venya mentioned learning dance at school and having weekly lessons with instructors.

Observing the children's playfulness and behavior, An couldn't help but admire how Benedek and Bella raised their five young ones. She had never seen such a large family where the children were so young yet incredibly independent. They knew how to entertain themselves, care for each other, and interact with strangers naturally. And to top it off, all five children were healthy and beautiful! The sight of this harmonious family was like a dream. Their organic lifestyle fascinated An. She wondered if Andras, who frequently visited this family, might be tempted by such a warm, cheerful, and ordinary family life.

***

Then it was time for An and Andras to bid farewell to Benedek and the five children. Bella had not yet returned home. Baby Aniska also picked some springtime flowers, gorgeously blooming, and handed them to Uncle Andras. Andras hung the flowers on the rearview mirror, then hugged and kissed the children goodbye. Venya discreetly slipped three walnuts into An's hands, which he had picked up from the garden. The sight of the five small children standing beside their tall father, waving their arms after the car, brought tears to An's eyes. Happiness could be so beautiful with such a simple organic lifestyle. What use were all the complexities of sophisticated technology?

But behind the steering wheel, Andras seemed pensive. From the moment he left Benedek's house, he said nothing more, just put on dark sunglasses and drove silently and slowly.

"They have wonderful children!" An broke the silence. "I will write about how an organic lifestyle can bring such great happiness. It is a real paradise. They don't need to search the world like me. I'm wondering, will you one day be so attracted to that lifestyle that you will marry a Hungarian girl, live in a beautiful house halfway up the hill, find your paradise, and stay there?"

"An, you know me. Don't say such things anymore."

"What happened?" An asked softly, sensing something strange in Andras' voice.

"I was shocked. I wanted to cry, but I couldn't. Maybe I need to stop somewhere."

"Andras, what is going on? If something is wrong, don't drive. Stop at a coffee shop, and we'll talk."

Driving a little further, Andras turned into a forest by the roadside. He pulled over, got out of the car, but didn't close the door. With his hands in his pockets, he stood staring deeply into the forest, still wearing his dark glasses. An approached him, gently hugging him from behind.

"Tell me what's going on, if you can," she whispered.

Andras turned around and held An to his chest. He lowered his face and pressed his lips to her hair.

Warmth spread. He closed his eyes, and after a while, he said, "Benedek and Bella are getting a divorce."

"You're not kidding, are you, Andras?" An pushed Andras away, to see his face clearly.

"I don't believe it either. I asked Benedek several times, but they have already decided - they will get a divorce."

"What about their five children? This is madness. The kids are so adorable! How could they separate them? What happened?"

"Not for a common reason," sighed Andras, "but because one day, Benedek's wonderful organic wife suddenly realized that she wanted to be a painter."

"Then Bella can just paint and continue the organic marriage like before..." An said, but she herself did not believe what she had just uttered. She shivered, feeling cold. She suddenly leaned back, the red shawl slipped from her shoulders, falling loosely across her chest.

"Bella wants to be an artist." Andras slowly wrapped the shawl around An's shoulders. "You know, an organic wife will stay at home with her husband and children 24/7, but a painter can't stay in one place, even if it's heaven. The painter will desire to explore everywhere, including hell. She no longer wants to devote herself to that organic paradise, her angel children can no longer tie her feet. And that's it: Whoosh! Everything suddenly fell apart! Shit! I wanted to curse, but didn't know whom to curse. Looking at my friend, forging a smile and talking, reassuring himself with the five angelic children who knew nothing about what was going on between their parents, my heart shatters..."

An's eyes welled up with tears. Who was she weeping for? For the innocent and immature children, for the depressed man coping with the sudden blow of so-called fate, or for the duality of women...

Perhaps, this was a harbinger, a reminder to both her and Andras, even burning in love, not to frivolously enter the elusive paradise of marriage. She would certainly be cautious, not to fall into the marriage trap, no matter how tempting it might seem.

CHAPTER SEVEN
THE SPECTRAL MAP OF JANOS HILL

At the ticket counter for the Libego cable car, Andras turned to An and asked, "In the afternoon, do you want to go for a walk, take a train run by children, or do we sit on the cable car again?"

"Cable car," An said without hesitation.

"I thought so," Andras smiled, playfully narrowing his blue eyes, "You're the girl who hangs in the air most of the time."

"I don't want to sit on a train driven by a child," An joked, "Who knows, as the train is going downhill, the children might be busy playing with each other and forget what they need to do. Why does Budapest let kids run this dangerous train line? Driving the train up and down the mountain is not a game, isn't it?

The Hungarians really know how to joke, or they might come from Mars!"

"Oh, I just showed you that track. The tracks and wheels are specially designed, like a mountain train in Switzerland, so that even if the train stops suddenly, it will not drift downhill," Andras explained. "So in case the children are busy playing and forget to control the train, the train will not have an accident like you imagine. Actually, the children run the train, but the driver is an adult."

"Whoever thought of that way to attract tourists is also too wise," An said.

"I think we Hungarians want to fool the kids, that they can do whatever they want. Hungary is small, but the Huns are great. That sort of thing. Probably because of our low self-esteem with our small country, we crave great and extraordinary things..."

"The Huns are really great," An looked at Andras seriously, "A small country with a small population, which has won 15 Nobel Prizes. Extraordinary. Who was the last Hungarian to win the Nobel Prize for Literature?"

"It seems to be the writer Imre Kertesz, who was born here in Budapest," Andras replied, raising his eyebrows slightly.

"Who is the next person?" An asked.

"Oh, how do I know?" Andras shrugged. "Possibly the craziest guy in Budapest..."

"Poet Andras?" An laughed, teasing Andras.

"Andras will win the prize if and only when An -- a writer and accomplice from Vietnam -- takes all the seats in that literary Nobel Prize Committee," Andras laughed.

"Okay, remember to share the prize with me," An crossed her pinky finger with Andras's. "I will go find my accomplices from now on."

Sitting in the cable car was an interesting experience. An had ridden cable cars many times in Vietnam, China, Japan, and Hong Kong, but they were always in closed cabins. She was quite surprised that in Europe, where caution and safety were always top priorities, they still maintained a rather adventurous cable car system like this. Surely on rainy and windy days, the system would not work.

"Lucky for you, today the weather is ideal, sunny and clear," Andras turned to An and whispered. "A few times before, I took this Libego cable car, it was foggy, and I couldn't see far. When you reach the top of the Elisabeth Tower, you will see a spectacular panorama."

"Wherever you go, the sun will follow you. What if I'm jealous of the sun..." An was joyful. "Was that poem made for me by poet Andras?"

"I just fooled you!" Andras smiled slyly. "Don't ever trust a man's words when he is in love, even the poems he writes in honor of your name."

"Unfortunately, I won today."

"Suddenly one day the Holy Spirit fell into the pot!" "That's what the Hanoians say about this case," An chuckled.

Birds were chirping from the oak trees below. An listened, inclining her ear to the sound of birdsong. She pointed the camera at the top of the oak tree on the left and took the shot. The click of the camera shutter sounded out of place in the tranquil, immense silence. An closed the camera; no matter how beautiful the scene was, she didn't take any more pictures. The electronic noise suddenly became a nuisance, troubling the immeasurable purity of silence. An was immersed in a moment of meditation. She closed her eyes, unknowingly awakening and gradually dissolving, as light as a cloud, invisible in the sky, drifting into the infinite universe.

Beside her, Andras was also silent. He didn't remember how many times he had taken the Libego cable car. He liked the feeling of sitting in the air and being pulled back to the top of Janos, the highest hill in the Buda hills. But right now, closing his eyes and letting the pure stillness possess his body and mind, was so refreshing. As an information technology expert, with a fast-paced, eventful life, Andras looked to poetry as a meditative solution for his overstretched brain in the world of technology. But more than poetry, in this moment of life, with this lady, he felt a new sense of life. Ultimately peaceful. He was completely free, spreading himself forever in the transparent, immortal air.

***

After about twenty minutes on the Libego cable car, they walked for more than five hundred meters to the top of the hill, where the Elisabeth observation tower was located, for a panoramic view of the fairy-tale city of Budapest and its suburbs. As he walked, Andras told An what had made the legend of this Janos hilltop. Queen Elisabeth of Hungary enjoyed picnicking up Janos Hill. Of course, Elisabeth was a beautiful woman. Because the women who went into the legend were very beautiful and seductive in the more and more exuberant imaginations of the descendants. It was the muse, not only of the king, but of the whole nation.

They pushed the king and the whole nation to go wild in the drunkenness of the lover. Drunk more than drunk the best grape wine in Lake Balaton. Drunk and crazy enough to win all 15 Nobel Prizes, the most greedy ratio in the whole world. And then later, even after the muse went to heaven, the Huns would still force her to live, on that peak, building a six-story memorial tower on top of Janos Hill in 1908. It made a tower. round spiral, built of lime and sandstone ivory yellow. A very attractive woman, at the top, beckoning the Huns to advance, if not by economic, scientific or literary achievements, at least set a record for drinking the most wine and swooning to the top of Janos hill...

An burst into laughter at Andras' witty interpretation of a historical site in Budapest. She knew well that, with him, she not only felt safe, reliable, and free to be herself in every way and every moment of life, but also laughed and laughed about his stories, about how he perceived everything around him, because of his slip-ups that deserved to be recorded in a book. This was the man who made her happy from the bottom of her heart, made her admire, was her endless inspiration to write, who made her smile even in her sleep. How much she loved him. She silently thanked God, Buddha, Saint, or any God, if there was any in the world, for bringing him to her life.

An gazed in awe at the tower that emerged before her. The ivory yellow sandstone color shone in the late afternoon sun. She suddenly remembered that she had to embrace this beauty that inspired her emotions when writing, so she took out her camera. Andras showed her the best angles. Then, jostling with many tourists, they ascended floor by floor to the tower of Elisabeth. An attentively looked and captured the wide scenes from the top of the tower.

Budapest stretched over a romantic terrain with rivers, mountains, hills and forests intertwined. An quietly watched the Danube river which looked as soft as a gray-blue silk from tower, and remembered the night on Géllert hill that day, the Danube seemed to change its color. Living in a place like this, one cannot help but be a poet like Andras, or at least nuture a poetic soul.

***

Catching a map displayed on the way down to the cable car, flanked by the station on the left, Andras pulled An's hand closer. He adjusted his glasses and began to look passionately at the map, muttering:

"This map shows the old route up and down Janos Hill that Queen Elisabeth used to take. Looks like it's different from the way it is now. I have never walked down the hill. Please bear with me, it's just because I love all types of maps. Every tiny zigzag like this is like a nerve in the brain, leading to something that may be obvious, but may be mysterious, hard to figure out."

"Why don't we try walking down the hill once?" An suddenly asked.

"Oh no, the road is very long, zigzag, about six kilometers, no joke." Andras said, eyes still glued to the map. "Besides, we already bought a round trip ticket to the cable car."

"Then you should study the map. I'll go over to the other side to take some more photos for documentation, that angle is also very beautiful." An pointed to the viewpoint built overhanging the slope. "When you finish your research here, you know where to find me."

Andras nodded, but didn't turn to look at An. He was absorbed in the map as if hypnotized. The red line drawing of Elisabeth's favorite downhill road seemed to darken, swell, and then expanded into a roadway through thick pine and oak groves. The road twisted and turned, iit was hard to see the next one, it's not clear if it's because of the fog or because the bend is covered by the pines. The fog grew thicker and thicker, making the road murky. Elisabeth had an entire entourage of guards by her side, but most of them were maids, only two large soldiers on horseback, one in the front leading the way, she could not see him because of the bend and the pine. concealed, the guy behind the rear couldn't even see it, because it was covered by fog. The maids that walked around her seemed to blur like ghosts from time to time. She reached out to grab one of the children's hands to reassure herself, but her hand caught on the mist. The right pine wing fell into a black abyss. She screamed in silence, turned around to ask for help, Andras was startled to see that she was An, he panicked and reached out to help her...

He suddenly shuddered, a cold shiver running down his spine, unsettling him to the core. His hand, trembling slightly, struck the glass of the protective frame surrounding the map. Desperate to avert his gaze from the mysterious object, Andras took a deep breath, attempting to regain his composure. Where was An? What had she said to him just moments ago? Ah yes, she had ventured to the opposite viewpoint to capture more images for her writing. Glancing at his watch, Andras realized they had a mere fifteen minutes before the cable car station closed.

On the other side of the road, all the tourists had departed, except for a man leisurely walking his dog downhill. But An was nowhere to be seen.

Anxious, he hurriedly crossed the road, heading towards the viewpoint where she had promised to wait. Scanning the area, he found no trace of her. Could she have excused herself to use the restroom?

After waiting a couple more minutes, Andras' restlessness grew exponentially. He tried calling An on the phone, but to no avail. He attempted multiple times, yet his efforts were met with silence. He then checked An's

Facebook and stumbled upon a picture she had posted from the Janos hill viewpoint, mentioning she had been waiting for him about 25 minutes ago. It meant he had been standing at the map for over twenty minutes, an unusually long time to study a mere public map!

Determined to reach her, he tried FaceTiming her, but the call remained unanswered. Could she be angry with him for making her wait so long? He knew her well enough to understand she was fully capable of leaving at any moment, despite his deep affection for her.

Andras scoured the area around the Elisabeth Tower, desperately searching for An. He even ascended to the sixth floor of the Tower, entertaining the idea that she might have returned to the top. But alas, she wasn't there either. He refused to believe that An would jump from the top of the Tower. Panic set in as he repeatedly tried calling and FaceTiming her, but she remained unresponsive.

As the weather turned colder, gathering clouds obscured Janos hill, adding to Andras' agitation. Had An vanished into the mist? Was there any way to ascertain her whereabouts?

An idea struck Andras. Surely, the cable car station must have security cameras. Embarrassed by the audacity of his plan, he felt compelled to discard all rules and regulations to protect An. He accessed his phone, connecting to the internet, and fumbled for a while until he successfully "unlocked" the security fence, gaining access to the data of the company BK, which managed the Libego cable car. He meticulously examined the footage of today's journey log, fast-forwarding and pausing until he found the scene of him and An seated in the cable car. He fast-forwarded again, this time stopping at the moment when he had paused at the map near the road leading downhill.

Andras abruptly halted the tape and stared intently at the image on the recording. There she was, An, standing at the observation point, her camera lens focused on the Danube river. But something sent a chill down his spine, and his skin crawled with unease. A man approached her, embracing her affectionately. And to his horror, that man was him! An turned and smiled at the imposter, nodding in response to something he said. They held hands and walked down the hill together, bypassing the cable car station and heading to the foot of the hill.

It couldn't be! Andras felt a sharp pain in his chest. Why was there another version of him, leading An downhill, hand in hand? He hadn't chosen to walk down Janos hill. This imposter must have deceived An! What dreadful intentions did he have?

"Oh God, An, why won't you answer my calls? Why did you follow that man without realizing?" Andras' panic intensified.

He disconnected from the Libego data system and desperately searched for the phone number of the BK security team, urgently calling them.

"Libego security, please go ahead," a calm voice responded on the other

end.

"Help me! My girl has been kidnapped by a stranger. He's impersonating me and taking her down the hill on foot. I'm sure they're still on their way. I bought tickets for both of us to go down by cable car, but that scammer led her down on foot. Oh, God! The path is so far and desolate, surrounded by forests. What will he do to my girl?"

"Calm down, sir. Please identify yourself. Where are you now? How do you know they went down the hill on foot?"

"I am Andras, and I stand resolute at the foot of Elisabeth Tower. I cannot fathom how I know they descended on foot, but I beseech you to aid me in intercepting them when they arrive at the passenger drop-off point by the hill's base. I shall shoulder the responsibility for this. Oh, please, do not permit my cherished one to be ensnared by the impostor who masquerades as me. I shall rush there with all the fervor my being can muster."

***

Andras dialed An's number, each ring slicing through his heart like a dagger. Clutching the phone in his hand, he darted down the pedestrian path, fueled by a sense of urgency he had never known before. Every ounce of vitality, the very essence of his life, infused his feet, which once so captivated An with the

mesmerizing whirl of traditional Hungarian dance, now twirling with desperate haste.

He ran, a torrent of anxiety coursing through him, determined to reach the part of the forest where that wretched man had led her astray. He beseeched the heavens not to let any misfortune befall her, or if it had already, to guide him to the spot where he could intervene and rescue her from impending peril.

As he sprinted, passengers and onlookers stared in awe and curiosity.

Even a dog, momentarily caught up in his fervor, followed him before eventually giving up the chase. Still, Andras pressed on, his heart pounding so fiercely it seemed ready to break free from his chest. Amidst the turmoil, the memory of that man tenderly embracing An haunted him. Oh, how well he knew that gesture, a gesture he had yearned to bestow upon her countless times with the fullness of his soul. Yet, was he truly capable of it? Why could the impostor replicate it with such ease, as if he were Andras himself? The resemblance was uncanny, right down to the white Armani glasses and the sturdy hands that held An with affection. It couldn't be real. So, who was he? Who rushed to claim An?

In that moment, Andras stumbled, finding himself once more before the enigmatic map. Goosebumps surfaced, unsure if he still stood in front of it or if he had been ensnared within its mysterious confines, running through an enigmatic realm.

Taking a deep breath, he grounded himself in the belief that he was, indeed, on the pedestrian path descending Janos Hill, sprinting to reunite with An, his beloved. Regardless of the confusion, regardless of the fear, he would press on, seeking her with unwavering determination, no matter the reality he found himself in.

Down the slope he hurtled, the world spinning around him, until he came to an abrupt halt. Before him sat a petite Asian girl in a red coat, her black hair neatly tied at the nape of her neck. An! He could scarcely speak, his gaze locked upon her intensely, fearing she might vanish from his sight.

"An, look here, a ladybug sits on the path," she said, pointing to a red ladybug clinging to a golden oak leaf. "I nearly stepped on it. I'll move it to safety."

Andras watched in silence as An carefully relocated the ladybug to the base of a nearby tree. His terror mingled with relief, knowing that she hadn't abandoned him. She was here, right by his side. But something felt awry.

"Why do you breathe so heavily, as if you just descended from the hilltop?" An inquired with concern, noticing the beads of sweat upon his forehead.

"I have indeed rushed down from there to find you," Andras panted, unzipping his coat. "Why did you go down this path without telling me, with that man?"

"Which man are you talking about?" An's surprise was evident. "You said you wanted us to walk down Janos Hill. We decided to forgo the cable car this time, remember? You even promised to treat me to fish soup at the nearby restaurant after the walk."

"Then who accompanied you on the descent?" Andras insisted.

"You did, silly! Why do you ask such strange questions?" An looked puzzled, gently touching his sweaty forehead. "Why are you so agitated? Are you alright?"

"Why didn't you answer any of my calls and messages? Where is your phone?" Andras' agitation grew.

"Answer your calls? I left my phone in my backpack. We were walking together, and you were chatting with me the entire time. What's gotten into you? Are you jealous of a ladybug?" An teased.

"I don't know anymore, An. Do you see me clearly? I'm Andras, and I called you on my phone. Please, take out your phone."

An reached into her backpack's hidden pocket and retrieved her phone to check. To her astonishment, she discovered numerous missed calls and messages from Andras, both regular and FaceTime. She began reading through the strange and alarming messages he had sent.

"What's happening, Andras? What is all this?" An tightly held his forearm. "I've been walking with you the whole time. I never left your side. This is really you, isn't it?"

"It is truly me," Andras affirmed. "I'm not sure anymore. It all feels like a nightmarish haze. I need to calm myself and reassess everything from the beginning."

They continued walking hand in hand, but Andras couldn't take his eyes off An. Had he experienced some kind of hallucination? Did it begin when he released her hand to examine that cursed map? Or was this a lesson, warning him never to let go of her hand, even for a moment? His restless heart found no respite, despite their tight grip on each other. His hand was sweaty, and she looked at him with concern.

"Hello, sir and madam!" A security officer in Libego's uniform stopped them at the passenger stop. "Apologies for the interruption, but may I ask you a question?"

"Yes," An replied, still puzzled.

"Do you have a loved one named Andras?" the officer asked. "Yes, he's right here," An pointed to Andras.

"I'm sorry, but another Andras called us, seeking our assistance. He claimed that someone was impersonating him and luring you away. He's in great distress," the officer explained.

An turned to Andras, who appeared far from trying to create a joyful scene for her. Confusion still clouded his visage. What in the world was happening?

"I am Andras," he stepped forward to speak finally. "I'll use my phone to call him again and verify my identity. Besides, I have other documents to prove..."

After a series of inquiries and investigations, the Libego security personnel allowed An and Andras to proceed, though doubt lingered in their eyes. Perhaps they were simply lost in a daydream. After all, a handsome young man and a captivating young woman like them could easily be ensnared by the whims of twilight.

An and Andras decided to forgo the fish soup restaurant at the base of Janos Hill. Instead, they hopped into a car and hastened to the Danube. There, they stood, gazing at the waning sunset over the river, enveloped in pensive silence.

Suddenly, Andras burst into laughter. "How can you laugh?" An turned to him.

"I've figured it out," Andras embraced her. "It's either the cursed map on Janos Hill or a figment of my imagination."

"Or perhaps you have an unknown doppelganger," An chuckled, pressing her cheek playfully against his chest. "Either way, it's an incredible experience.

Oh, the enigmas of Budapest."

"After this ordeal, I'll pen a short story to rival yours," Andras whispered, kissing her forehead. "This chilling tale is worthy of prose."

CHAPTER EIGHT
ON HEAVEN'S HILL

"At 6 o'clock this evening, be at Heaven's Hill. I'd love to pick you up there," read Andras' message. An felt a twinge of disappointment. She had thought Andras would drive all the way to the house of her acquaintance at Thang Long Market to pick her up. But instead, he suggested she make her own way to Heaven's Hill, wherever that may be. An called him to confirm, and Andras chuckled, explaining that it was his personal nickname for Gul Baba, a quaint street nestled on the Buda side of the Danube River. Everyone agreed that it was the most beautiful little street in Budapest.

An smiled, finding Andras' rendezvous message now tinged with romance. Indeed, she had been living in Budapest for over a month and had not yet set foot on Heaven's Hill, which was somewhat regrettable, wasn't it?

Besides, despite her repeated visits to Budapest for months of exploration, the city, known as the fairytale capital, still had a few magical surprises up its sleeve.

An had been away from Andras for 9 days, embarking on a journalistic assignment at Thang Long Market, a Vietnamese market in Budapest. She was conducting a series of reports for Lao Dong newspaper in Vietnam, focusing on the life and trade of Vietnamese people in one of the famous Vietnamese markets in Europe.

Andras suggested that she not stay away from him for too long. He proposed to pick her up daily in his car, take her to the market to meet her compatriots, and then he would head off to his tech company for work, returning to Thang Long Market at the end of the day to bring her back to his home on Bartok Bela Street in the old quarter. However, An declined, claiming she wanted to stay with a fellow countryman at the market to listen to more of their life stories and gain deeper insights into their way of life. Besides, despite her reluctance, An knew she needed to spend some time apart from Andras. After being close to him for so long, his affectionate nature might make her feel compelled to be completely his, so she felt the need for some distance. But she kept this to herself and didn't reveal it to him.

Though she loved and missed him deeply, yearning to embrace him each morning upon waking in the midst of his vast collection of books, she had to restrain that feeling. She had to overcome the instinctual desire to become his woman, to be forever entwined by his side. She had her own path to walk, to write and explore her unique capabilities, to scrutinize the world closely. She

couldn't allow her love for Andras to tie her down here, no matter how beautiful and sweet that bond might be.

Look at her compatriots in Thang Long Market; they felt as if their lives had changed upon reaching the European paradise, yet they clung and toiled day and night. But they couldn't look up, couldn't lift their heads from the piles of goods and daily struggles to know where Budapest's Heaven's Hill was, and perhaps, they had passed by it multiple times without recognizing it as such.

They had spent their whole lives here, yet not once dared to step into a helicopter to soar through the skies and behold the panoramic view of where they willingly lived and died. They lived in Europe, yet their culture remained thousands of miles apart from the culture they clung to. An would never choose to live a life of mere attachment, a seemingly ordinary existence. For she was An, and her life was a journey, seeking authenticity in every moment of living.

***

An intended to take the bus to the place where Andras had arranged to meet her, but Tuyet, her friend from high school, insisted on driving her there. An had been staying at Tuyet's place for 9 days, and Tuyet's life story was nothing short of extraordinary. Tuyet, however, had no idea where Gul Baba Street was, despite living in Budapest for over a decade. She had to follow the directions provided by the navigation app. As they neared the location, Tuyet stopped the car by the roadside and said:

"I'll have to drop you off here. My car can't make it to the foot of that Heaven's Hill you're going to. Just walk along this street for about a hundred meters, then turn right into a small alley. Walk another two hundred meters, and you'll find Heaven's Hill. Hopefully, you won't get lost."

"Oh, I'll follow your directions, and if I do get lost, I'll seek help from 'Google map' – An replied, waving goodbye to Tuyet.

"Hey, An," Tuyet refused to drive and rolled down the car window to call out to An, "Do you know what I'm thinking right now?"

"What are you thinking?" An asked.

"I wish I could travel the world like you," Tuyet replied. "Why don't you then?" An inquired.

"I still need to earn money, support my two sons' education, buy a third house for rental income, and save some money for old age when I can no longer work... Oh my goodness!" Tuyet lamented.

"Well, you can put aside those everyday worries, pack your bags, and hit the road today. In essence, most ordinary people don't spend more than one-third of their earnings on themselves. However, the fear of not having enough and the concern for others always bind us, making us work tirelessly until death, forgetting our own souls, even losing them long ago without realizing it," An said, sounding like a philosopher.

"You talk like a philosopher, don't you? Alright, I'm leaving now; otherwise, your philosophy will tempt and eventually pull me out of the dizzying whirl of my life," Tuyet said, then suddenly sped away.

An followed Tuyet's directions for a while before stopping, taking a deep breath. It seemed like the Danube River was very close, right in front of her. It was strange that she could smell the fresh scent of water. Or was she just imagining it? Or was Heaven's Hill somewhere nearby, veiled from her sight?

Just then, memories of the Red River embracing her beloved Hanoi, where she had lived for over two decades, flooded back. She remembered that desperate night when she couldn't sleep upon hearing the news about Andras.

An had rushed to the river, standing alone on Long Bien Bridge, utterly lonely but somehow comforted. The river carried the weight of muddy alluvium, its dark waters flowing silently beneath her, as if soothing her despair and turning it into lines of empathetic poetry:

Wandering through the realm of longing, Immersed in deep pain,

The Red River misses the Danube, Silently hiding its profound waves.

Loneliness deepens the nostalgia, Sleepless nights waiting and hoping, Verses thirst for fiery passion,

But... only ashes remain.

An was astonished by this strange occurrence; she had never written a poem in her life. She had never thought she would churn out such verses. But perhaps, it was the Red River that wove those lines on the surface of its dark waters, consoling the young woman in that uncanny moment.

And precisely at this moment, with the blue Danube before her eyes, the nostalgia for the Red River surged within An. It was peculiar how two rivers, thousands of miles apart, had become soulmates. An found liberation from the anguish of futile contemplation when she realized that happiness and love were about intimacy and harmony of souls, not mere physical proximity. A heartfelt conversation could penetrate to the very core, in silence and in wordless language. The Red River had imparted a profound lesson, during that night when she engaged in a solitary dialogue with the flowing waters.

***

An suddenly halted her steps as a delightful and alluring fragrance enveloped her, wrapping her in gentle tenderness. The scent of roses! She was immediately drawn in by the aroma, moving forward curiously, regardless of where it might lead her. After about thirty steps, she came to her senses. Before her was a vibrant red rose carpet ascending upwards. A small hill covered in roses that took her breath away. In the middle of it, a wide pathway, about two arms' width, beckoned her steps. An hesitated whether she was allowed to ascend this path. Why such quietness? Why was no one here? Where was Andras? Nevertheless, An continued onward, as if in a dream.

And there, she stopped before something extraordinary. Amidst a sea of crimson roses, were snow-white roses arranged to form her name: AN, ANH YÊU EM, in Vietnamese. It could only be Andras. The romantic, passionate, and mad Andras of Budapest, who could conceive of such magic and turn it into reality. An's heart skipped a beat, as if it wanted to drop, a sensation so intense that she had to raise her hand to her chest to hold it.

Just then, Andras appeared, as if descending from the heavens, right in the midst of Heaven's Hill. He knelt before her, arms outstretched. Tears welled up in An's eyes, and she rushed into his embrace.

"Oh, Andras, how could you do this for me?" She finally managed to stammer.

"Because I love you. Because you deserve the most beautiful thing I could create in this world," Andras whispered, gently kissing her cheek. He loosened his embrace and guided her further up the hill.

An heard applause echoing from below the hill. She turned around to see a group of people taking photos with their phones, laughing cheerfully. Some were starting to ascend the rose-covered hill.

"I had to ask them to stop using Heaven's Hill for half an hour to wait for you. Fortunately, they cooperated with me. This is an unprecedented gesture.

Perhaps not just for you, but also for Budapest and the random passersby, all of them will receive a gift," Andras said, his eyes sparkling behind his glasses.

"Oh, you're simply too much. So, where's my diamond ring?" An teased

him.

"Even if I were to dig up all the diamond mines on this Earth to obtain the

largest diamond to present to you, my proposal would still be meaningless. Nothing can bind you, not even my love," Andras paused, looking into An's eyes.

"You truly know how to steal my heart. But I feel guilty after this overwhelming happiness. With these roses, you'll go bankrupt!" An shook her head, speaking.

"How can I go bankrupt when I have the 'Father of Roses' supporting me?

If you go up to the top of Heaven's Hill with me, I'll introduce him to you," Andras said, pulling An up the hill, who reluctantly stood there, gazing down at the rose-covered Heaven's Hill. She would cherish this moment for a lifetime when Gul Baba Street adorned itself with roses for her.

***

Andras extended his arm, pointing to a statue of a man wearing a turban on his head and dressed in traditional Turkish attire.

"That's the 'Father of Roses.' He brought rose seeds to Hungary hundreds of years ago, and his romantic spirit has enriched life here," Andras explained.

An approached, reading the plaque attached to the statue, then turned back to Andras, surprised. "In reality, he was an invader. Why would Hungary erect a monument to commemorate an invader?"

"That's the truth of history. We respect historical value, and in the end, Hungary still belongs to the Hungarians. Erecting his statue also carries that significance," Andras spoke simply.

"In Vietnam, we don't do that. During the time of Northern invaders, they sought to assimilate the Vietnamese, bringing their own music to teach us. But we transformed and improved it into our own national music, and the Northern men didn't have statues erected like Gul Baba here," An explained.

"That's the difference in how we perceive historical and cultural values," Andras mused. "But we still share a common point. Despite being invaded and occupied, ultimately, the Vietnamese remain Vietnamese, and the Hungarians remain Hungarian, nothing else. That's the authenticity of our identity. It makes us eternal."

***

The two returned to Heaven's Hill once again, this time descending the slope to reach the Danube River's bank. An walked slowly, reluctant to leave this "paradise."

"An, do you know where my eternal paradise is?" Andras asked. "Where?" An hazarded a guess, but still inquired.

"Right here, at this very moment, with you by my side, doing everything together," Andras replied.

"But you know I won't be here forever with you. Even in this paradise, even though I may travel the world, no other man can create a paradise as beautiful as Budapest for me. I'll return to the earthly realm, to Vietnam, to the Red River, and from that native root, I'll continue my boundless journeys," An replied.

"And I don't think about what will happen," Andras shrugged. "I'm fully present in this moment. Dreams or paradises are what I'm creating in the present. However I dream, I live that way."

"It's the most intense way of living that I've seen in you. It's something I haven't possessed yet, but I'll practice. Not dwelling on the past, not worrying about the future, knowing who I am and doing what I want right now. Living every minute for the present. That's living in a paradise of my own making, not the paradise of any saints or deities," An expressed.

"Many people think that they must live righteously to wait for their moment to enter paradise after death. Waiting like that is exhausting, and who knows if the deity might change their rules just as we're about to enter the gates of paradise," Andras grinned, his enigmatic blue eyes sparkling. "That's why from a young age, I've lived intensely and created my own paradise in the present. It's genuinely quite simple."

"It doesn't seem simple to me, as almost everyone else thinks differently from you. They believe they have to meet certain conditions or criteria to enter paradise. What's your secret then?" An asked.

"Authenticity and being completely present in the moment. That's all there is to it!" Andras held An's hand as they walked along the Danube's edge, like lovers from previous lifetimes, like young lovers of a thousand years hence, to feel deeply the eternal flow of the water, like time, like the love of two souls.

CHAPTER NINE
AT THE BOTTOM OF ECSTASY

Andras suddenly woke up. He heard "something," quite indistinct, that roused him. The faint light from the balcony door seeped into the common living area, letting him know that the sun had risen. It must be five-thirty or six in the morning. Perhaps, as on any regular day, he was woken up by habit, nothing out of the ordinary.

He yawned and stretched his body comfortably. But he liked to think that there was something peculiar that woke him up this morning, while still in the drowsy state between sleep and wakefulness. He listened attentively for a moment, but the space was completely silent. After a while, he heard the sound of a car running on Bartók Béla Street below, but he believed that it wasn't what woke him.

Finally, he decided to sit up, climb down the wooden ladder connecting the bunk bed and the wooden floor with nimble, precise movements without needing to look. The wooden steps had become so familiar to his feet, almost as if they reached out to welcome him in his dream wanderings.

He wore his pajamas -- the thick white cotton pants with large red and dark blue checkers and an ivory-colored cotton pull-on shirt. The elastic muscles seemed to disappear, making him look quite slender in the loose outfit. Out of habit, he walked towards the small toilet on the right side of the apartment, above which a stained-glass picture of a plump lady blowing a gentle breeze towards the East was hung. And he abruptly stopped.

He heard the sound of water splashing rhythmically from the large bathroom. An must be taking a shower using the hand shower. He suddenly felt a tightening sensation in his lower abdomen. She must be standing naked under the warm, trickling water. He could imagine the misty bathroom with the steamy air and An's tender body, smooth skin, wet, flowing black hair cascading over delicate shoulders, sticking to her small, round breasts. An alluring haze in the clouds, in the mist. He felt as if he was melting right then, turning into droplets

of warm water cascading endlessly from the hand shower, covering all of An's seductive, soft, and captivating bare body.

He took a deep breath, suppressing the mad desire to rush to the bathroom door, to embrace her wet, fresh body with his lips, his tongue, his hands, everything, to savor every inch of her glistening skin, shimmering in the hazy mist of water.

He didn't see the pair of slippers used for walking inside the house in front of the bathroom door. He swiftly walked towards the main entrance of the apartment, searching for the small white cotton slippers in the shoe cabinet, bringing them back, and placing them right in front of the bathroom door. This way, when she stepped out of the bathroom, she could slip her feet into the slippers. Then, he hurriedly entered the toilet across from the bathroom to change his sleeping shorts, discovering that they were wet. He couldn't let An see that embarrassing stain at the front of his shorts.

He didn't know how long he could maintain "The Budapest Oath" between him and An. Love without sex, the pure spiritual love "model" was indeed pristine, but perhaps he hadn't reached the lofty "realm" yet, so he continuously struggled with the ancient desires that surged within him, the lasting cravings in every man since the time of "living with hair in the hole," when people lived together in caves, and men could forcefully push their desire onto a woman, tearing her apart, to satisfy their sexual urges at any time. But he was living in the 21st century, or maybe the 22nd and beyond, with An, the girl he loved, coming from the mysterious, distant East, and more than love, he revered her like a saint on a high pedestal. He could only look up to her and pray, with pure desires and then stepping back, never being able to embrace and indulge in physical desires. He always had to struggle, caught between treating An as an icon or devouring her as a delicious treat. In that struggle, he measured the depth of his own culture.

To drive away the turmoil that spread from between his thighs, to his heart, to his brain, Andras boiled some water and made lotus tea. An liked to have hot lotus tea every morning, and she brought a lot of this tea from Hanoi to Budapest. Andras did the same; it was strange that they didn't use coffee in this elegant and somewhat frivolous Europe. The two young people, one Asian and one European, enjoyed drinking lotus tea in quiet contemplation like two old Vietnamese men leisurely sitting at a sidewalk tea shop in Hanoi, as a way of appreciation and preservation of the Eastern values. The ancient custom of

Hanoi had crept into this romantic corner of Budapest. Or perhaps it was a disguise for a Western-style debauchery hidden somewhere inside them.

The bathroom door opened, and An stepped out. She wrapped her upper body in a soft white bath towel, with a smaller piece covering her head, hiding her black hair. She was taken aback to see Andras sitting at the dining table in the middle of the kitchen. The bath towel suddenly slipped, prompting An to quickly cover her chest and tightly hold the towel. Andras smiled and turned away from her.

"Go on, I haven't seen anything!" Still facing away from An, Andras called out.

"I thought you hadn't woken up yet. Sorry," An hurriedly said, hugging the towel to her chest, and she rushed into her bedroom next to the main entrance.

Andras suddenly craved for Shisha. He stood up, waiting for An, and he took a few puffs of the tobacco while waiting. He hoped it would help him shake off the particular sense of haze in his mind this morning. Now he understood; "something" woke him up, and it was his mysterious ancient instinct, whispering and tempting him towards the most easily surrendered moment. "Something" hidden deep within An's hot body, loosening under the warm water, right inside his house, was calling him to explore it fully. And the moment the bath towel fell off when she saw him sitting there was a challenge that seemed difficult to overcome. But he had overcome it, and now he would reward himself with a Shisha session.

***

An used the towel to dry the upper part of her body. She couldn't fully concentrate on the task at hand. There seemed to be something bubbling inside her, demanding to be released. She tried to suppress it and continued to bend down to dry her legs. When she reached her thighs, she stopped, feeling nervous. Something uncontrollable seemed to leak out from between her thighs. It flowed out warm, right at the moment when she saw Andras sitting there, his gaze burning through all her defenses. She needed to go back to the bathroom to rinse between her thighs. But she felt embarrassed; if Andras saw her going back to the bathroom, he would figure it out. That would be terrible.

She looked around and saw a pack of wet tissues on the nightstand by the head of the bed. She quickly pulled out two pieces, cleaning up the mess, tightly rolling up the wet tissues, and carefully putting them in the small trash bin with a lid under the table across from the bed. Her face was flushed, and she took a deep breath and exhaled, trying to calm herself down.

An herself had safeguarded "The Budapest Oath." It was an extension of the symbol she had created for herself when she decided on the path and fate she wanted. No man had ever made her feel powerless with such inner desires as Andras did. But it was also the first time she unexpectedly saw her body betray her own will. Perhaps she hadn't anticipated the situation when Andras woke up, and she stepped out of the bathroom with his fiery gaze tearing down all her barriers. The door guard named "will" was floating in a blissful feeling from the warm water vapor, so it lost its vigilance, leaving her vulnerable to the natural instincts bubbling from within, from the depths of her body's cage. In just an instant, with a strange touch of the gaze, she had surrendered herself to Andras, the boy born from the blue Danube River, from the rich and historical Buda region. Once the cage was unlocked, what should she do? With the sense of urgency between her thighs.

An sat on the edge of the bed, crossing her right leg over her left. The sensation intensified as her young thighs touched each other. An quickly stood up; she needed a strong cup of lotus tea to regain her composure. Oh, Andras, why did you look at me like that?

An opened the wardrobe, amidst the row of Andras's neatly hung shirts, there was a short section of her own dresses hanging. She chose a red cotton dress with white flower patterns and hurriedly put it on. During her stay in Budapest and at Andras's home, he had given her the largest bedroom in the apartment and allowed her to use his wardrobe. An guessed that he usually slept in this room, which explained why the large wardrobe was almost overflowing with clothes. On top of the large bed, there was a mid-sized bunk bed, elegantly connected together with a soft, curved ladder. Since An arrived, Andras had slept in the bunk bed connected to the bookshelf in the common area. Every time she saw him climbing up to the bunk bed or lying on his stomach on the upper bunk talking to her, she felt his mischievous childishness still intact in this young man. And she enjoyed that playful side of him. Surely none of his colleagues at the multinational tech company could know about this aspect of him, as they saw him as the fiercest tech expert in the company and a tech star in Europe. An

couldn't help but smile when she thought about it. And she felt more confident as she stepped out of the bedroom.

***

An didn't see Andras sitting in the chair near the dining table a moment ago. She noticed a freshly brewed pot of lotus tea that was still steaming. She sat gently in the chair opposite the one he had occupied before, pouring herself a cup of tea into a silver-rimmed glass. In Budapest, young couples didn't drink tea in porcelain cups like in Hanoi. The fragrance of tea wafted, the subtle scent of lotus occasionally tickling her nose. An took a light sniff of the tea, her eyes following the thin white smoke that gently dissipated on the surface of the tea. She took a small sip. The tea had a refreshing and delicate taste, quite different from the strong bitterness of the tea on Hanoi's street corners.

After finishing the first cup of tea, she poured herself another. Andras still hadn't returned to the kitchen. The apartment remained quiet, but she suddenly noticed a new fragrance gently wafting in. After a moment of tranquility, An tried to guess what this fragrance was – elusive, sometimes pleasant, but when inhaled deeply, it had a lingering and intoxicating allure.

Could it be that Andras was smoking Shisha? He only smoked it when he felt strong emotions and wanted to savor it for a longer time. And afterward, he might write a new poem, or a philosophical essay would take shape. An stood up and walked into the common area. Indeed, Andras was sitting half-reclined in a soft beanbag in the corner, just below the ceiling of the hallway leading to the tall bookshelf, lost in the smoke. His blue eyes squinted at An through the thin white haze, half fascinated and half curious with pleasure.

"Try it," Andras got up, reaching for another Shisha mouthpiece from a lacquered wooden box on the table and handed it to An.

"I've never used this before," An shook her head. "I probably can't handle
it."

"That's your thought, but reality may be different. Let's do a little experiment. Take a puff to see if your thoughts are correct. Besides, smoking this is not as harmful as cigarettes."

An sat down next to Andras, holding the mouthpiece he offered, hesitating.

"Actually, I hate all kinds of smoking, regardless of whether people conclude that it's harmful or not. In Hanoi, I lost a spiritual mentor whom I deeply respected. He died of lung cancer after smoking for 45 years. He passed away at 65, at the peak of his scientific research career, vibrant and radiant..."

"There's nothing to condemn about that," Andras looked at An, his gaze still somewhat squinted, as if the smoke had dissipated. "He had reached the peak, and perhaps some stimulant he used for 45 years contributed to that brilliance. Long or short life doesn't determine the quality of life or the happiness one achieves."

"I was by his side, taking care of him during his final stage. It was incredibly painful, both physically and mentally. I can accept losing him, but I can't accept the terrible suffering he endured," An sighed.

"Actually, that suffering helped him," Andras said softly. "How so?"

"When the pain became unbearable, he might curse life or grit his teeth to endure it, and at that moment, he might desire to die. Dying to escape life's burden. Then, death would not be as terrifying as we usually think; it would be liberation, granting him freedom. What could be more pleasurable than freedom? Those who have died, their souls now soaring freely above, might be looking down at the living with pity for their loss of freedom and suffering."

"You're speculating. How can you be so sure? You're not him," An objected.

"Oh, that's the dual nature of all things, all phenomena," Andras suddenly leaned closer to An, sniffing like a curious puppy. "Have you just drunk the lotus tea I brewed?"

"Yes," An replied. "Why? Can you smell it on me?"

"And the scent of lotus too," Andras said, "You find the fragrance of lotus pleasant, don't you?"

"Of course," An replied, "Otherwise, why would I drink lotus tea every

day?"

"Do you like mud then? Can you put fresh mud in a pot and brew a drink with it?"

Andras continued to inquire.

"Disgusting!" An exclaimed, "What are you trying to do?"

"There's no game here; it's just the truth. Without mud, there would be no lotus. The most fragrant flower arises from the foulest mud. Everything, every phenomenon, no matter how dreadful, possesses certain value, worthy of appreciation."

"So, you mean I should love even your flaws, right? Cherish your bad habits too?" An smiled mischievously, her eyes playfully glancing at Andras.

"In the portrait article you wrote about me in the Hanoi Literature Journal, you once praised me as a talented poet, a mathematician, a top-notch tech expert, a handsome and romantic young man. Very attractive," Andras chuckled, "but you haven't seen a demon in me."

"A demon?" An raised an eyebrow.

"Earlier, when you stepped out of the bathroom, that demon broke free.

You were nearly in danger. Luckily, I managed to confine it again," Andras said, avoiding eye contact with An.

An also looked away. Suddenly, her tongue felt dry, and her breasts were sore. It was only now that she realized she had forgotten to put on her bra. Her nipples stood defiantly, pushing up against the layer of red cotton fabric with white flower patterns. She awkwardly folded her arms across her chest, stood up, turned her back to Andras, and walked dreamily toward the balcony door.

"You've managed to restrain one evil demon, but there is another demon within you, and it may well be beyond your control and yours too," Andras said.

"I want to be a pure, beautiful saint on the pinnacle. Pure, chaste, and holy. You must gaze at me throughout your life without being able to touch me. But, oh dear, right here, right now, that female saint seems so tasteless. And the demon lurking inside me is alluring, full of bewitching powers. And I will choose the demon right now, if you can't stop it."

An leaned against the balcony wall, pushing hard. She lowered her head, looking down at the sparse flow of vehicles on Bartók Béla Street, her hair cascading over her cheeks, indistinguishable from her teardrops. Suddenly, she had a peculiar wish – to fall freely from there, to fall anywhere, even into hell, as long as it meant letting go, as long as it meant falling...

CHAPTER TEN
JAMES BOND'S TEARS

From the Danube riverbank, An crossed a bustling street running alongside the river and entered the lobby of a community building. Glancing to the right, she saw an elevator going up to the upper floors. Stepping into the elevator, she hesitated as she looked at the buttons. Besides the ones marked with familiar directions like "up" and "down," there were Hungarian words challenging her understanding. An chuckled to herself and pressed the button for the highest floor. When she didn't comprehend the Hungarian words, she relied on her instincts. Instinct was a wise deity within An. This deity had never played tricks on her. Whenever she faced difficulties and didn't know how to handle them, she always remained silent and let her instincts guide her. Then, she simply followed its lead.

The elevator opened up to a pathway leading uphill. An looked up and saw a statue of a goddess at the top of Castle Hill. Andras had instructed her that when she saw the Goddess, it meant she was on the right path. He would be waiting for her at the Hungarian State Opera House. Tonight, they were going to enjoy a traditional dance performance called "Sky through Father's Window" with a contemporary touch. Andras emphasized that if she got lost, she should call him, and he would immediately know her location and come to find her.

For someone like An, a seasoned globetrotter who had roamed over thirty countries alone, getting lost might seem laughable. She could easily turn on her phone, use the Google Maps app, and instantly have the route laid out.

However, in beloved Budapest, where she had just arrived and was staying for the first time, with a man she loved more than herself, using Google Maps felt like an insult. It was akin to asking a matchmaker to find the ideal man for her to embrace for a lifetime. An was from Hanoi, but she considered herself a global citizen who could find her way to Andras, her paradise, without any assistance.

Climbing the last flight of stairs towards the hilltop, An took three more steps and paused. A whole fairytale world unexpectedly unfolded before her, leaving her heart to skip a beat in awe. A magnificent panorama of palaces, churches, and ancient fortresses revealed themselves all at once, shining resplendently as if gilded in the fading evening light, connected to each other in a grand display along the Danube river. Walking through the ancient city, she approached Matthias Church, like a massive balcony that mesmerized travelers, inviting them to admire the distant Pest bank. An imagined herself standing on a wide arc of a golden balcony surrounding the hillside, and she, too, was glowing in the fading golden light of the sun. The sun also seemed regretful to bid farewell to this fairytale land.

Wandering through the evening of Budapest, where the ancient city leaned towards the river, where every thought swayed like intoxicated notes from the fragrant echoes of Balaton wine, was how An reached the soul of Budapest, seeking to understand how she could live and love in this place.

***

Andras looked up at the grand entrance of the Hungarian State Opera House. Immediately, he spotted the petite figure of the Asian girl in her maroon coat. He smiled and rushed towards her like a gust of wind. She always made his heart dance with joy, and his feet felt like dancing too. If not dancing, then he'd run. Andras was indeed a breeze, a strong wind carrying the breath of the Danube. An merely needed to take a step, and she would be enveloped in his warm embrace.

"Such a sophisticated lady!" Andras playfully admired An after helping her remove her coat inside the theater's lobby. "I'll find the most elegant and distinguished gentleman to suit you."

Andras stretched his arms out, holding An's coat in his left hand. He looked like a tech-savvy prince. Comfortable blue jeans, a long-sleeved red T- shirt, and prescription glasses on his eyes. He had rushed straight from the IT company to the theater. Unlike An, he spent no more than two minutes choosing his attire and makeup to fit the theater setting.

"Even without clothes, you'd still be the most handsome man," teased An. "I can't take my eyes off you. Other men are just extras in your presence."

"Oh, please!" Andras winked and led her to the coat check in the left corner of the theater's lobby.

An wanted to keep her phone, so she took it out of her wristlet and then handed the wristlet to Andras, along with her coat, to be checked along with the audience's belongings. In theaters in Hanoi, there were no "acts" of checking bags and coats before entering the auditorium. Perhaps in Budapest, art appreciation was seen as a ritual, needing to shed all constraints and entanglements to feel light, relaxed, and pure while stepping into the sacred sanctuary of art.

"Are you sure you need your phone?" Andras cautiously asked An. "No photography is allowed during the performance."

"I know!" An pouted. "I need the phone for communication; what if I get lost without you!"

"Lost in the theater? Impossible," Andras said in surprise. "I'll always be by your side. But okay, keep the phone if you want."

***

The performance "Sky through Father's Window" began. The actors wore traditional Hungarian costumes, dancing and singing ancient folk songs in the warm brown light of nostalgia. The male dancers moved with sticks, symbolizing the opening and closing of windows. The image of a busy mother, always on her feet but with a serene face, trusting in her husband's sheltering presence, the image of a quiet husband, burdened with the responsibility of being a pillar, and a growing son full of inner struggles: how to become a true Hungarian man? The boy looked at his father with fear, hoping his father would hint at how to become a man, a real Hungarian man. The father sat there, his gaze fixed outside the window, a lonely, solitary gaze aimed towards the sky.

The boy tried to fix his gaze in that direction, repeating. And at that moment, both Andras and the boy looked out together, sharing the deep loneliness and fears of the father, who also saw himself in the form of his son, looking up to his father for guidance on how to become a true Hungarian man. All three gazes converged into one straight line, connecting Andras, the boy, and the father, running through the window, aiming at the sky, and repeating. The profound pain and genuine pride of the ancient Hungarian man continued to connect through an invisible thread. Andras was deeply moved, his heart aching for the boy, for the father, for himself, and tears streamed down. With his decision to remain single for life, Andras might escape the father's position, but he could not escape the position of a son. In front of him, an old silver-haired woman reached out to comfort her husband. Andras wanted to lean on An, but she remained

silent beside him. She didn't understand Hungarian, perhaps she hadn't fully sensed the spirit of the performance.

Yet, even if she could understand and embrace him, as the Hungarian woman sitting in front of her husband was doing, it would still be a story between

Hungarian men, between father and son, a thread connecting generations without intentionally binding women. Women were always placed on a pedestal to be worshipped, not to be restrained.

Andras exhaled, relieved, and reached for An's hand, holding it firmly.

She released her phone onto the seat, holding his hand wholeheartedly.

***

An was drawn to the dance and music. She admired the Hungarian art of dance, especially the performances by the male dancers. However, she couldn't understand their singing. She vaguely felt something arising from the changing tones and expressions of the dancers, but couldn't fully grasp the emotional spirit. She felt excluded because she didn't understand Hungarian. At this moment, she felt like an outsider, a stranger in the heart of Budapest. She wouldn't be able to fully penetrate the soul of Budapest without comprehending the language here. A strange sense of loneliness flooded her, taking hold of her, and she felt connected to the Hungarian women, the wives in aprons bustling in the corner of the kitchen, completely untethered from the invisible threads of Hungarian men. And she shed tears. Just then, Andras's hand reached for hers, trying to connect.

An understood that Andras, the James Bond of Hungary, the extraordinary man of the tech world, the daring pilot, the skilled rock climber, and the enigmatic mathematician, was also shedding tears. Tears were contagious, and they could connect when language became inadequate. At that moment, an idea arose in An's mind. She would learn to master Hungarian, surpass this unexpected challenge, with just Andras's hand to hold. Strangely, with just a hand to hold, the extraordinary James Bond of Hungary could impart strength to help her transcend her own limitations. When she committed to becoming part of Budapest's life, she couldn't rely solely on English with Andras; she needed to understand Hungarian to penetrate the soul of Budapest, in its native language.

His tear fell precisely when she felt alienated, when she was about to lose herself in the spiritual realm. In the different spiritual realm of Hungarian men, her love sometimes struggled and drifted. She appreciated his tolerance and unspoken understanding.

An wandered around Andras's spacious apartment to find him and wish him good night before going to bed. She saw him sitting slumped in a chair, his expression inscrutable. She approached, embraced him, and bid him good night. As she was about to get up to go to the bedroom, he held her back.

"An, I feel drained, parched!" Andras stumbled for words. "I'm very thirsty..."

"Perhaps the play has taken all your tears," An said. "I'll make up for it."

After taking a sip from the glass of water she offered, Andras shook his

head.

"A million glasses of water can't compensate for a single tear shed. An, don't pretend not to understand. I'm speaking to you in English, not Hungarian. Are you letting me die of thirst or something?"

"I have to run away," An thought. "Otherwise, I'll be lost in the labyrinth of chaotic physical desires."

An turned away, intending to close the bedroom door. But she couldn't escape the storm of Andras. She collided into him, and his thirsty lips found the sweet source. An no longer resisted her instincts. She let go, allowing the torrent of love to overflow.

Two souls merged in the endless current of the universe, whispering a hymn in the language of the cosmos.

When Andras released her lips, gently embracing her on his chest, An understood that he wanted to stop at the boundary of commitment, with the

pledge to Budapest. With this, neither of them had led each other astray. Because their love was too sacred and pure, especially at this moment.

He gracefully opened the bedroom door and closed it after wishing her a good night.

An sat on the edge of the bed, her heart still overflowing with the torrent of emotions from the kiss, so deep, so sweet, so selfless. She was grateful to him. She needed to tell him that. She would send him a very sweet message.

An searched her wristlet for her phone, but it was nowhere to be found.

The phone had disappeared. Scouring her memory, An was certain she had left it at the theater.

The phone, an inseparable object for her—a creature somewhat dependent on the virtual world during wanderings. In the fifteen years since she got her first phone, she had never lost it. Yet, here in Budapest, where she met the deepest love of her life, she had lost her phone.

That surely held a special meaning. An took a deep breath and pulled the covers over herself. Time to sleep; she'd think about retrieving the phone tomorrow. Even if it was permanently lost, it didn't matter, as long as her soul didn't wander away in the tears of James Bond.

CHAPTER ELEVEN
BLUE FOOTPRINTS

An woke up drowsily. The hazy sensation made her want to continue immersing herself in sleep. Where was she sleeping? This initial thought was quite familiar to a girl who had traveled to many countries and never had trouble sleeping in unfamiliar beds.

She rolled back and forth on the bed, which was very spacious. It was the bed in Andras's apartment bedroom!

An suddenly smiled with joy. She had just woken up in Budapest. How long had she "occupied" Andras's bedroom? Well, she would figure it out when she had the time. With her eyes still closed, An reached her hand toward the bedside table to check the time on her phone out of habit, but her hand hit a tube of lotion, causing it to fall to the floor. She opened her eyes, fully awake now.

An bent down to pick up the lotion tube on the glossy brown wooden floor. Andras was thoughtful to have placed the lotion tube right beside the bed for her. The dry, cold climate in Budapest was in stark contrast to the hot and humid atmosphere in Hanoi, leaving her Asian skin in need of moisture, always requiring lotion. This tube of lotion had run out, and yesterday, Andras had placed a new one next to it, which she hadn't used yet. An was grateful for his silent care. Every small action of his melted her heart.

"You haven't used up that lotion yet. Why did you buy a new one?" An playfully scolded Andras.

"You never put it on? Isn't it finished by now?" Andras asked. "I thought it would've been empty last week. This is body lotion, meant to be applied all over after bathing."

"But I usually take showers at night. After showering, by the time I get to bed, I'm already half asleep and can't resist falling asleep without calmly applying lotion." An explained her lazy self-care habits.

"If you're feeling lazy, I can apply it for you. I won't be lazy with that!" Andras laughed and winked.

Recalling that situation, An also smiled, imagining the feeling of his hands applying lotion all over her body. Oh, no, she shouldn't entertain that thought. It was naughty! Such thoughts immediately disturbed her mind.

She needed to edit those disorderly thoughts. An wasn't just a savvy editor for a Fashion magazine; she also constantly edited her own thoughts.

And at that moment of editing, An jerked upright. Last night, when they went to watch the dance performance at the Hungarian National Theater, she had left her phone on the seat there.

***

An hurriedly walked to the common area. She was fully awake now. Last night, it was too late, and she didn't want Andras to worry, so she didn't tell him about forgetting her phone at the theater. She had planned to ask him to call her phone early this morning. If an honest person found it, they would answer the call and return her phone.

But Andras was no longer there. He must have already gone to work at the tech company.

An sat down on the couch, put her index finger to her mouth, and nibbled gently. She worried. If her phone fell into the wrong hands, what could happen? She didn't lock the screen, so someone could access her Facebook, Gmail, Zalo, WhatsApp, Viber accounts, and use the "Hey, I'm in Europe, and I've lost all my money. Please transfer 1000 Euros to me so I can buy a ticket back home..." script to deceive her acquaintances. Or they could dig up her private information, bank account details, and wipe out her account balance.

But what was the use of worrying while sitting here? The "editor" in An spoke up. If she worried, she would be imprisoned by her own fears. In the past, Bui Giang didn't have a phone, a bank account, or a Facebook account... and that middle-aged poet still "roamed Saigon, Cholon, going up and down, a lifelong

wanderer." Besides, An was a globetrotting writer with friends like Andras here in Budapest, and wherever she went, she had friends. Her circle of friends was something no one could steal from her, so why worry about a lost mobile phone?

But now she had two choices: One was to stay at home and write the next chapter of the romantic novel she co-wrote with the novelist Istvant; two was to go out and explore Budapest alone. Three was to write a short story for the literary magazine. She had honed her writing skills to be very fast and could simultaneously work on three different books without getting their ideas mixed up. This was a spectacular ability to surpass herself, unlike in the past when each novel took her three years of struggling to write. Now, with focus, she could complete a novel in three months while still writing two other books and articles. The nickname "Literary Sorceress" that people bestowed upon her seemed to have penetrated her subconscious, and she had truly become a sorceress when writing. Thinking of that, An smiled, feeling a bit proud.

She chose option Two. Despite having lived in Budapest for over four months, An was used to being chauffeured by Andras whenever she went anywhere, or when he was busy, he would always buy train or bus tickets for her and give her instructions before she set off. Today, she would wander aimlessly, without any predetermined plans. She wanted to explore everything unexpectedly, leaving behind blue footprints along the way.

An was a "walking angel." Walking stimulated the imagination and creative abilities of a writer, and it cost nothing in terms of tickets or fuel, did not contribute to environmental emissions, and was beneficial for her health, keeping her feet strong on the long journeys. Because of these various benefits,

An called her walking activities "leaving blue footprints on the earth."

***

In the fast-food restaurant on the 6th floor of the tech building, where tech companies had their offices, Andras was having gulyás while also scrolling through Facebook to check his inbox messages. He hoped to receive a romantic or humorous message from An, like she usually sent him. He referred to it as a refreshing ice cream after lunch. Indeed, An's messages always made him as happy as enjoying an ice cream on a summer day. "Better to enjoy it before it melts."

But today, Andras didn't get to enjoy that refreshing treat. An hadn't messaged him anything in his inbox. He checked her recent updates to see if she had posted anything this morning and was taken aback. A peculiar post appeared about three hours ago: "You forgot your phone at our place last night. Please come to the Hungarian National Theater at... and meet the receptionist to get your phone back." After a few seconds, Andras understood the situation. He immediately called An's number.

After two long rings, a man answered the phone. Andras confirmed that it was his girlfriend's phone and arranged to meet in six hours to retrieve it. He thanked the person who had kept An's lost phone and asked him to check the battery. If it was running low, please charge it to ensure they could communicate.

Andras felt a bit puzzled. Could An not know that she had left her phone at the theater last night? But she probably knew by now, so why didn't she inform him? She could easily use the computer, contact him through Facebook, and let him handle this for her. Yet, she didn't do any of that. What was she thinking and where was she now?

Andras clenched his fist and unconsciously flexed and stretched his fingers. Oh, perhaps the habits of a patriarch and control were surfacing again within him. Or was it because in his past life, he was born in Hanoi? Hanoi men always felt confident because they knew where their women were going and what they were doing... Budapest men also wanted to know, but they pretended not to, fearing the truth.

***

From Bartók Béla Street, An walked towards the Hungarian Parliament Building on the Pest side. It was past nine in the morning, but this proud old street still seemed like a princess who loved to sleep in. The street was sparse, and occasionally a car would whiz by, but it couldn't dispel the dreamy atmosphere in the cool autumn air of the temperate region. Breathing in the crisp air, An wondered if Andras had ever walked alone on this street, heading towards the Liberty Bridge, just like she was now. Maybe not, because he lived here and was already too familiar with the place. No matter how beautiful and charming the scenery was, he couldn't find a reason to walk over six kilometers from home to the Parliament Building like she did.

Approaching the beginning of the Liberty Bridge, An stopped to admire the grandiose complex of hotels on the left. Inside was the luxurious Gellért Thermal Bath, built since 1918. Andras had once taken her there, inviting her to relax and play chess on the water surface. But An declined, using the excuse of being on her "red flag" days. Thinking about it, An couldn't help but chuckle, recalling the trick of waving a thin sanitary pad in front of the object of desire to suppress the surge of sexual desire. In most cases, it was quite effective for men who could control themselves.

This was the first time An walked across one of the nine ancient bridges over the Danube River. This blue-colored bridge could be seen from Andras's fourth-floor balcony on Bartók Béla Street. An took a few steps on the bridge and stopped, looking up at the bronze statue of the Turul bird on top of the iron pillar. The morning sun reflected dazzlingly on the gold-plated national emblem next to the famous mythical bird of Hungary. Truly, when she was rushing across the Liberty Bridge in the car with Andras, she couldn't calmly admire the statue of Turul like this. But dear heavens, at this very moment, she remembered how much she knew about Andras. She saw his presence everywhere she went, even when she was alone. Every word he said, whether in jest or sincerity, echoed in her mind like poetry, repeating over and over. It seemed as if Budapest itself was Andras, and as a result, it became the loveliest and most beautiful city in An's eyes.

She leaned against the railing of the bridge, gazing as if she wanted to capture with her eyes the picturesque image of the fairytale-like city on both sides of the gentle Danube River. It wouldn't be long before she left this place, even though she wished she could stay. The Red River, with its red, tumultuous flow during the rainy season, kept calling her back. Those conflicting thoughts made her legs feel weak.

To escape the heavy emotions within her, An meditated by walking slowly and counting each step. She focused intently on counting. Each step was a gentle touch, a kiss on the beloved blue bridge. In total, there were 999 steps, and An had reached the Pest shore. She remembered that while crossing the Long Bien Bridge over the Red River, she also counted her steps and had to take 5043 steps. An couldn't easily pass up the pleasure of walking across a bridge, whether it was one spanning a river, stream, canal, or even two mountains – it was an adventure of connection.

An turned back to admire the blue bridge once more before strolling along the Pest riverbank, heading towards the Hungarian Parliament Building.

However, for some reason, she only looked at the Parliament Building for less than twenty minutes before walking to the riverbank, seeking a place to sit. There, she sat alone, facing the blue waters of the Danube, with the wind playing with her hair while her mind continued to think of Andras without respite. She no longer tried to edit her thoughts but allowed them to wander freely before this river. Her thoughts about Andras kept repeating, nothing new, yet incessant, making her heart feel exceedingly tender.

How could she stop these thoughts about Andras from whirling and surging within her every time he wasn't around? It was a river of intense desire, as powerful and turbulent as the Red River during the flood season. And she was in the middle of it, struggling to swim upstream or downstream, but neither seemed to lead to escape. Because, in truth, she didn't want to escape.

Because she knew very well that the only way to escape was to marry him. At that point, her intense desire would be satisfied, it would slumber, and it would die!

She wanted Andras, the most beautiful poet in Budapest, to remain a longing, a dream she could never reach.

Or perhaps, she would write a book about him? And her soul would be purified?

***

Upon opening the apartment door, An saw Andras standing there in astonishment. He looked more like a dashing James Bond spy than a dreamy poet. He swiftly grabbed her and, in an instant, lifted her with his strong arms, carrying her out to the balcony.

"Tell me where you've been all day, or else I'll let you fall," Andras threatened, placing her on the balcony's edge.

"I won't tell, but I need a truce before I fall," An laughed, reclining comfortably on the balcony, releasing her grip on Andras's neck.

With her chin raised to the sky, her eyes fixed on the end of the street where she could see the Liberty Bridge, her lips were dangerously close to his chin.

He tightened his arms around her waist. Their lips were almost touching, but he didn't kiss her. He savored the alluring scent, teasingly withdrawing from her lips, feeling his heart racing faster, his legs and body tensing.

"Put me down, and I'll tell you. I can't take it anymore," An pleaded softly.

Truly, she wanted to lean up, just a little, to brush her lips against his. But she wouldn't give in. Her chest felt sore and tender. Why did he come up with such a terrifying way to torture her?

Carefully, he set her down on the balcony railing, as if handling a child. "I called you, but no answer," he finally said, sitting down next to her. "You always know how to scare me."

"I left my phone since last night," An admitted. "I think I forgot it at the theater. So when you called, did anyone pick up?"

"Here it is," Andras pulled the phone out of his pocket and handed it to An. "Luckily, the theater's staff kept it for you."

An suddenly leaned up and kissed Andras's right cheek.

"Yet, I thought this phone was dead. Are people in Budapest so honest and kind?" she said.

"Not necessarily, but those who set foot in the theater are all angels," Andras smiled.

CHAPTER TWELVE
IN THE HEART OF BUDAPEST

With undisguised admiration, An watched Andras' skillful hands maneuver the steering wheel, turning and pressing as he navigated up a steep hill. He stopped the car just as they reached the hilltop.

"Are you allowed to park here?" An asked hesitantly.

"Anyone is allowed if they are capable," Andras replied, with a familiar touch of arrogance whenever he did something out of the ordinary. "Don't get out of the car yet; let me check if it can drift backward down the hill."

An sat still, but she wondered why Andras didn't drive the car all the way to the top of the hill and park it there safely.

As the question arose, she couldn't help but smile. It was precisely this kind of daring adventure that had intoxicated her, like a skilled IT expert in this

European city. If Andras did something ordinary like everyone else, he wouldn't be Andras. Moreover, he was a top-notch mountaineer, so having his car precariously perched near the hilltop was probably his peculiar kind of pleasure that she could understand.

Andras opened the car door on her side. As she was about to step out, he bent down, swiftly grasping her right foot while holding a shoe brush in his right hand, and started cleaning and shining her shoes. Gently placing her right foot down, he continued with her left shoe.

"These shoes seem to have accused their owner of playing around outdoors all day," Andras murmured. "Budapest is dusty now, but it still can't compare to Hanoi."

An burst into laughter, utterly defeated by Andras' unexpectedly romantic act. Not one of the Hanoi boys, even if they pursued her for a hundred years, could come up with such a way to remove dust from a pair of shoes that had traveled countless miles with the elegance he displayed.

Andras stood up straight, offering his left hand for An to step out of the car. His hand was thick, warm, firm, and trustworthy, giving her a sense of protection like that of a father's hand. If she had to choose any part of Andras' body that made her feel the most affectionate, it would undoubtedly be his hands. Right now, she wanted to close her eyes, pressing her cheeks gently against those hands for a long time.

"Well, let's go, shall we? Hanoi, please accompany us to the birthday party," Andras said cheerfully.

While An was lost in thought, Andras had already changed into a new outfit – a white shirt with dark blue stripes. He looked youthful and radiant, unlike his rugged, dusty appearance from their outdoor adventure. How could anyone be so swift?

***

Once, as he drove An around the old quarter of Hanoi, zigzagging through the streets, Andras told her that he felt as if he had been born in Hanoi or had lived here in a past life.

"Every year, I promise to return to Hanoi during springtime," Andras said enthusiastically. "I miss Hanoi so much. Hanoi's heart already beats within me."

"And you have a Budapest heart," An playfully added. "Now, where does your Hanoi heart reside?"

Andras drew closer, hugging An tightly. She remained still, feeling his chest, his heartbeat. Strangely enough, she didn't feel embarrassed that he could sense her heart beating beneath her bra, and she felt confident accepting him in complete silence and harmony.

"Do you feel it?" Andras whispered. "The Hanoi heart is on the right side.

And everything you desire, I can sense, belongs to the realm of possibilities."

An smiled. It was Andras' birthday today, his 36th, and she believed this was the most brilliant age of his life. She had secretly prepared a stunning surprise gift with his closest friends. Andras had been curious and pestering her all day about the evening's plans, but she stubbornly refused to reveal anything.

She led him to Soroksari Street and entered a large restaurant overlooking the Danube River. Andras paused before the sign "Hanoi City" hanging at the entrance. His face lit up as he stepped into the hall, where the familiar scenery of Hanoi appeared warm and inviting with its brown wooden tables and chairs, Dong Ho paintings, Bat Trang ceramics, oil lamps, and red silk flowers. What made it even more special was that the staff were all young Vietnamese men and women dressed in traditional ao dai, with warm, friendly smiles on their faces.

Andras was nearly speechless as the birthday melody played, and his closest friends, all wearing ao dai with sashes tied around their foreheads, approached him with large trays covered in red silk, as if it were a traditional betrothal ceremony.

- "Andras, open it up!" Csaba, Andras' colleague from the technology company, exclaimed.

Andras stepped forward excitedly, flipping the red velvet cloth covering the first tray: a bundle of fresh, juicy lychees, the Northern Vietnamese fruit he craved the most.

The second tray held Thinh's pho, the best pho in Vietnam according to his taste, and he could eat two bowls in a row.

On the third tray: a small book. Andras opened it to find a collection of poems by An, with a dedication to him – "James Bond of the land of the Danube."

Csaba walked over, pretending to snatch the poem from Andras' hand.

The beginning of Johann Strauss' "The Blue Danube" played, and Csaba began to read the poem slowly:

"You can make time stand still Over the beloved skies of Budapest

Riding the wind god, quieting the Danube waves

The Freedom Bridge stretches to catch your smiling eyes Beyond time, you become immortal

Born for me, in the green years of longing

You stand there, a woman atop a mountain peak Letting go of time, for the laughter of happiness."

Andras stood there, still, astonished. The power of surprise welled up, bringing tears to his eyes. Csaba pushed An towards him.

There she was, both familiar and strangely new. They seemed to stand at the pinnacle. An, a writer from Hanoi, had now become a poet in Budapest's heart!

"You were right, Andras, that within each person lies a poet. I am grateful to you for seeing that in me and for helping it come to light," An said.

"How could you do this?" Andras finally spoke, his voice choked. "A whole Hanoi in the heart of

Budapest. It truly is a mystery. Next time, when we return to Hanoi, I will show you a few secrets; you'll be surprised."

"Secrets of Hanoi that I don't know? Are you a spy?" An teased.

"Oh, I forgot that I am Hungary's James Bond! I've had missions in Hanoi," Andras replied playfully.

"Alright, let's be a bit more practical, you two," Csaba interjected. "There are missions you both need to execute right here in Budapest. Why not turn this event into a wedding?"

"That's a great idea, Csaba, but we are not getting married!" An smiled.

"Why don't you get married?" Csaba looked surprised.

"If we get married, we might end up divorced. But if we don't get married, we'll definitely never divorce," Andras explained.

"Then let's raise a toast to celebrate Andras' birthday, to celebrate the immortal love of two clever artists who refuse to let marriage strangle their freedom."

"Freedom forever!"

As the empty wine glasses were placed on the table, Csaba exclaimed, "I think we should lower the romantic drama curtain and move on to reality. Before we finish the three bowls of pho, I'll tell An a secret. Budapest's poet Andras indeed writes beautiful poems and has written a lot, so much so that his pen has run dry. So, I doubt your poetic declarations and oaths from Budapest. But this Andras here, we are close friends and colleagues, I'll lend you my pen!

Absolutely free!"

Laughter erupted from the group of friends. And as Andras playfully raised his fist, An took shelter behind him. She knew that after the first glass of wine, there would be humorous performances and endless laughter. Hungarians were all outstanding comedians, and they often used alcohol to satire everything in life, dethroning all idols.

CHAPTER THIRTEEN
MEDITATION AT VYSEGRAD

Enchanted by the wandering jazz tunes from the music player in the car, An's dreamy eyes gazed towards the right, following the flow of the Danube as Andras skillfully maneuvered the car like a circus performer up the hill, heading towards Vysegrad, once a treasury of precious jewelry collections and crowns of the Hungarian dynasty.

Late autumn evening, the sun had set behind the distant mountains, yet it still cast a crimson glow on the sky before fading entirely. The road up the hill was tranquil, as if all people and vehicles had suddenly vanished, leaving only the car carrying Andras and An, gliding like a soaring bird around the hill. The sensation of flying was exhilarating, and An wished to leave all thoughts behind. She slowly became transparent, weightless, almost intangible. Like the most extravagant jewelry and royal crowns that this place once held, guarded and preserved, they too had become intangible.

The car stopped. Andras turned off the engine. As he reached his hand towards the safety lock on the right, his hand brushed against An's left leg. An suddenly snapped back to reality and instinctively moved her leg to the right.

"You think the car designer is a heavyweight womanizer, intentionally placing the lock there so that whenever you reach for it, you accidentally touch the beautiful lady's leg. Unsafe contact," An said with a laugh, seemingly unconcerned about any touch or desire.

Even if, at this moment, Andras were to take advantage of the deserted hilltop and lean her onto the car, exploring a body that remained a mystery to him, it would have no effect on her. She had detached herself from her own self.

But he did not do that. Perhaps he, too, had transcended himself, free from any earthly attachments. He opened the car door, extending his hand to help her out. The air was cold, and her hand was cold, yet she did not shiver. Maybe she had dissolved into this space, where ordinary sensations no longer existed. Andras led her to the side of the fortress wall. They did not admire the towering Vysegrad behind them; instead, they looked down at the Danube below, where the graceful bend of the river intertwined with the foothills, creating a marvel.

He pulled her towards him and sat down against the fortress wall. He placed her on his lap like a delicate little doll, his hands warming hers. They sat in silence, meditating on the hilltop. The wind rose from the river, gently embracing them, passing through them peacefully. They, too, dissolved, merging into one, like a breeze, like the air, flowing in the endless stream of the universe. From their two individual beings, something unique and eternal was born in the universe, as natural as the moment it needed to come into being, in the flowing source of harmony.

"Tell me, what is the book you most want to write in your life?" Andras asked quietly.

"It's called 'Living in Harmony.'" "When will you finish writing it?"

"I don't know. I write it with my very life, and I don't know when my life will reach its conclusion. That remains a secret."

"A book that is never written is an immortal book," Andras said. "But can you at least tell me what the core of the book will be, or its most secret aspect?"

"It's the miracle from within me. I seem to have a third eye. I can see the souls of all things and all people, and I embrace living with all of them, like swimming with the current, without trying to possess, control, or impose my desires. When I desire something, it naturally comes to me without much effort. I have everything, yet I possess nothing."

"I understand now why while most writers and poets are chained to a spot, suffering from poverty, afraid to go anywhere for lack of money, language skills, or other conditions, you travel the world and write, not for awards, not for fame, not to be understood by others," Andras said pensively. "It's truly miraculous."

"And even simpler, I eat without slaving away in the kitchen, love without demanding marriage or possessing a partner, believe in old age without needing children, breathe freely without paying a price… I know how to be happy with all the gifts life brings."

"Even death?" Andras suddenly asked, his hands touching her cheeks, gently turning her face towards him.

"Death is a profound gift of life, the source of rebirth. I don't need to wait for it, because it will come at the right moment, and I'm always ready."

"Why do you think like that?"

"Because, at this moment, here, not haunted by the past, not worrying about the future, I look deeply into myself, calm and serene, allowing my true self to fully reveal itself to you, to me."

As if something had shattered, perhaps they had become one another. Andras was liberated, he kissed her with emotion, tenderly, deeply, grateful. Those lips were as cool and pure as an invisible breeze.

CHAPTER FOURTEEN
SOLACE OF THE
FOREST NIGHT

Szentendre at night was rather deserted, despite being a tourist spot recommended by travel websites and adventurous travelers who shouldn't miss it after making the effort to visit Budapest. There must have been some mysterious reason why Andras brought An to explore Szentendre at this time of the evening. The land lay on the enchanting curve of the blue Danube, which had silently called out to her for a long time. But it wasn't until living in Budapest for over a year that An finally arrived in Szentendre, an ancient town with a historical connection to Hoi An in her homeland.

An had come to Budapest not as a tourist, of course. She lived and wrote here, now, while deeply in love with a young man from Budapest. In the unique experience of a traveling female writer, she had lived in various cities across Europe, but nowhere had she cherished as deeply as Budapest. She had lingered in Budapest longer than any other place, enjoying thrilling experiences with an adventurous young man who always kept her surprised. At the same time, her writing allowed her to delve deeper into the spiritual life of this land.

Andras extended his hand for An to hold. The narrow and steep street, paved with rugged blue stones, challenged each step in the dim light of street lamps. Everyone had to walk slowly on Szentendre's ancient streets to avoid stumbling. An almost swung into Andras' strong arm. She wasn't afraid of falling; she just wanted to nestle against him. She leaned on that warm, sturdy frame and followed him without bothering to look down at the road. Instead, she looked up at the rows of lanterns hanging across the street, emitting a gentle light through beautiful pastel fabric shades. Elegant and charming, it lacked the overt allure and enigmatic Eastern mystery that enticed curiosity like the red lanterns in Hoi An.

The sound of their timid footsteps in the night was clear. There was absolutely no sound of engines, no tourists in sight. It seemed as though only Andras was holding the hand of a petite Vietnamese girl strolling around the narrow streets of this ancient town. They stopped at the top of a hill, facing an ancient church with pronounced Baroque architecture, clearly visible in the typical winding path at the entrance. The church stood gracefully in a faint white light, and An leaned into Andras, silently admiring the elegant and soaring architecture. Suddenly, Andras pointed down to the ground:

"Look."

A dark shadow stretched across the ground, and right beside it was a slender, short shadow.

"Look at your shadow," Andras said. "It looks like his rib cage!"

An immediately stepped away from Andras. She took three steps forward and stretched her legs, but her shadow remained quite modest.

Andras stepped forward and embraced her from behind. Now, only his shadow was on the ground.

"You've swallowed me whole!" Andras exclaimed.

"That's wicked!" An playfully punched Andras' back but didn't want to slip out of his embrace. Oh, his arms were so warm.

"I like this unified darkness. It's confusing, but it works a wonderful magic with the light from the lamp, blending us into one complete entity," Andras said.

"On a spiritual level, we've already been one ever since we fell in love," An said. "So, the harmony of our souls reflects in which dimension, with light or darkness?"

"Your question is so profound, but I can't give a precise answer right now.

Maybe it's in the dimension of spiritual space."

"Spiritual, huh? So, how does this harmony work?"

"Through brainwaves. For example, when you encounter danger, I'll feel scared. When you think of me, remember me, my heart will flutter like the Danube's ripples meeting the wind..."

"Are you speaking as a scientist or a poet, Andras?" An reached up to playfully flip Andras' collar, asking.

The poet Andras didn't respond, but he lowered his head and gently kissed her lips.

***

They had dinner at a seafood restaurant specializing in fish dishes near the central square of Szentendre. The restaurant was alluring with romantic candlelight flickering on the vintage musical instruments scattered on the walls and ceiling. The brass horns gracefully displayed their undulating curves, the violins exuded elegance, and a large harp stood in a corner, exuding a delicate aura. All of them were silent, an unexpected calm before erupting into the most intense and passionate symphony.

The seafood restaurant exuded the familiar aroma of fish soup with chili pepper. Fish was a dish that Andras could eat all his life without getting tired. Perhaps it was one of the sources of his strength, enthusiasm, intelligence, and admirable creativity. An was also becoming familiar with his culinary delight. She focused on her dish, savoring the slow sweetness of the fish and the distinctive spices.

The characteristic sweet and spicy taste of Hungarian traditional cuisine gradually penetrated her taste buds.

"All the food in this restaurant is organically grown," Andras said after taking a sip of a rare white wine made from grapes grown in Szentendre's only vineyard. "You can rest assured that if we maintain an organic lifestyle and consume organic food, we'll live to be a hundred."

"So, how can one always think in an organic way?" An raised her head to ask him.

"Being true to oneself. Thinking, speaking, and acting as one," Andras replied.

"Even with bad thoughts, evil intentions?" An teased him.

"That's a matter of choice," Andras asked back. "When you see a caterpillar clinging to a leaf, do you catch it or let it eat the leaves?"

"I suppose I would choose to write poetry," An stepped back. "Like you, my mission is to create the finest verses rather than getting entangled in meaningless matters. And I hope poetry will make the world a better place."

***

Andras drove swiftly through the dark forest, the road deserted amid the woods, enveloping An with the feeling of being swallowed by the night. She felt

an inexplicable thrill, perhaps due to the allure of the darkness, the forest, and the unknowns lurking in the shadows.

Suddenly, Andras slowed the car down. "Seems like there's a police car ahead," he whispered. "I hope they won't notice us. I had a glass of wine earlier. I think I'm fine to drive, don't you think?"

"You seem okay to me, but the police might think otherwise," An shifted slightly. "Have you ever been caught by the police for driving slightly intoxicated?"

"Not in Hungary. Hungary is not only beautiful but also quite lenient with peculiar folks like me, which is why I chose to live here. But when I used to live in Germany, I got fined a couple of times for parking in restricted areas and driving too fast, too dangerously. I never drink when I have to drive. This time, I did it because of you. Being with you makes me so happy and carefree, I didn't think about the consequences."

"And you're blaming me?" An teased.

"You're not responsible for that mistake. It's just that you're too enchanting, and I couldn't resist, so I made a mistake willingly. I've been thinking like this since I became conscious. Oh, thankfully, the police turned to another road," Andras said, immediately speeding up. The car shot forward like an arrow on the empty road.

***

"Andras, can you stop the car somewhere? Let me walk in the forest for a while," An asked hopefully, turning to Andras. She couldn't resist the temptation of the nocturnal forest. She had never been to the forest at night, but with Andras by her side, she wanted to experience it.

"Strolling in the forest at night isn't very normal, but we're both quite unconventional. The Szentendre forest has many charming paths for walks, and there are even some attractions, but I've only visited them during the day. At night, all services are unavailable. There's no one in the forest at night. Only wild animals or ghosts," Andras stopped the car at a parking area by the road. They found a path leading into the deep forest. An curiously looked into the right direction of the path, where the dim light of the street lamp only illuminated a few roots of ancient trees, followed by the mysterious silence of the dark forest. An could smell the damp earth, the scent of leaves, and the moist air. The chill seeped deeper as they walked further into the heart of the forest. Suddenly, the

oak and beech trees seemed to sway in the cold breeze, which was laden with moisture.

"Oh, it looks like it's going to rain," Andras said, looking up at the night

sky.

As if responding to his words, a sudden rush of raindrops threatened to approach from behind them, the first hailstones falling onto the pebble-strewn path, shining strangely in the distant street lamp light.

"Oh, it's hail!" An exclaimed, half thrilled, half apprehensive, looking at the sparkling ice pebbles under the lamp light. She quickly pulled the hood of her coat over her head.

"Here, the first hailstones are always small. It's subarctic rain; very cold.

We need to find shelter quickly," Andras explained.

Seeing an information board indicating a sheltered area, Andras pulled An to seek refuge while waiting for the rain to subside.

Curiously, An looked at the fragments of ice gathering under the shelter of the information board. She nudged them with the toe of her shoe; they didn't seem to melt. The cold was becoming more and more penetrating with each passing moment, and An shivered.

Andras took off his coat and draped it over An's shoulders. "If you wear this, you won't shiver anymore. We don't know when the rain will stop, and the more it rains, the colder it gets. I'll run back to the car, then drive here to pick you up. Don't go anywhere, just wait here, and if there's anything, call me on the phone."

"I left my phone in the backpack in the car!" An said.

- Is that so? But it's okay. I'll be back quickly," Andras said before hastily running off.

Left alone, An sat down and picked up some hailstones in a pile under the shelter. Instantly, her fingers became icy. She wiped her hands on her pants and then stood up, stuffing both her hands into Andras's coat pockets. The waterproof coat was quite thick and warm; she pulled it up to cover her lips and nose, inhaling deeply the warmth lingering on the collar. She regretted agreeing to wear his coat, knowing he was now facing the cold rain with only a high-

necked T-shirt on. He would be soaked and feel terribly cold. Oh heavens! Why was she so slow to react?

At that moment, she shivered, feeling a sudden chill. A horrifying sight appeared before her, after a fierce lightning and the chilling roar of thunder, white rain streaks tangled around a face of the forest with black, tangled fur, a menacing mouth gaping with jagged teeth. A short roar echoed, and the street lamp shattered. Everything plunged into darkness. An screamed, but her cry was stifled in her throat.

A hand of darkness brushed past her right shoulder, and she jerked away, running for her life. She rushed wildly through the pitch-black forest. The cold water droplets pierced her skin, seeping into her bloodstream, running straight to her heart. The thick trunks of oak and beech trees continuously collided with her, causing her to fall, get up, run, and fall again.

"Andras!" An desperately called his name in vain.

Her blood was slowly thickening, freezing, her limbs growing numb, losing sensation. An suddenly realized a gigantic shadow of horror rushing toward her. She stumbled and tried to run, but her legs were now completely paralyzed. Right at that moment of falling, a bright thought flashed in An's mind, overriding her panic, that if she died, the last image Andras would remember of her would be An huddled in his wide, leafy green coat, just like her shadow fitting perfectly into his when they stood in front of the Szentendre church, entwined in the interplay of darkness and light. It would be a perfect death, with her.

That was An's last thought before all sensations faded away.

***

Andras struggled to open the car hood to check. He couldn't start the car.

He wrestled with the idea of trying to start it again or running back into the forest to find An. This damn car chose the perfect moment to fail during the cold forest rain, threatening his little girl.

Andras attempted to start the car again, but to no avail. He grabbed his phone and called for emergency roadside assistance, then dashed into the forest, running toward An. A strange and anxious feeling filled his heart. How long had he left her? Was it half an hour? He hoped his coat was enough to keep her warm. Andras ran through the rain, which hit his face, stinging his eyes. But the

coldness he felt wasn't just from the harsh subarctic rain; it was a deep, eerie fear. He didn't know what it was, but it was haunting.

Suddenly, he spotted something—a patch of leaf green standing out against the brown forest floor. His coat and An were there! Andras rushed forward, dropping to his knees to lift his little girl. She was pale, her eyes half- closed, freezing cold.

Andras frantically kissed her face, as if trying to infuse her with his life, his warmth. But she didn't respond. The cold and the darkness of the forest had almost taken her away from him. Andras lifted her up, holding her tightly against his chest, and he ran, ran away from the treacherous darkness, away from the panicked loss, away from the seductive lure of the night, defying the arrogance of mankind.

In the darkness, they needed to be one. Like his large shadow, encompassing her small one, in front of the church, they would be safe.

But An didn't want that. She had willingly stepped out of safety to experience the night forest, to let her small shadow get lost in an endless darkness, regardless of the consequences. An adventurer's soul, the most primitive that remained on this planet. She had thrown herself into the situation created by both the Almighty and the demons.

But Andras didn't want An to be lost like that, even though he knew it was an immortal moment. He ran frantically, carrying her, racing against himself, surpassing the gigantic shadow of the forest night, defying her demon- driven passion, to bring her back to his world, to his burning desire to live.

CHAPTER FIFTEEN
RETURN TO ETERNITY

Restlessly, Andras wandered through the Szent Istvan hospital which was nestled at the heart of the Ninth district, along the serene shores of Pest. For an entire day and night, he lingered in the corridors of the bustling emergency room, consumed by worry. An was receiving attentive care from a team of distinguished doctors, led by the renowned Vietnamese professor, Professor Hoang Lam, and he fellow Vietnamese colleagues.

Ironically, Andras had vehemently protested when A decided to stay at the professor's house in Budape for a week. In an attempt to please him, she only pa a brief courtesy visit to the professor at the hospi and in doing so, had to abandon her original plan writing a memoir about the accomplished Vietnam scholar in Budapest—a city of remarkable beaut Central Europe.

Andras wasn't driven by jealousy of the sixty-yea professor. He simply couldn't bear the thought o woman he loved dining at another man's hou mere five kilometers away from their own. An was relieved when Andras prevented her from to Professor Hoang Lam's house, and she q reached a compromise. Such decisions were reasonable when the young couple was engulfed in love, unwilling to part even for a few minutes.

Now, An's life rested in the capable hands of Professor Hoang Lam.

The allure of the nighttime forest and the enigmatic darkness beckoned An into the depths of the woods at Szentendre. Lost and disoriented, she was caught in a torrential ice rain. It was Andras who found her, unconscious and shivering from the cold. As the ambulance rushed them back to Szent Istvan hospital, Professor Hoang Lam regarded Andras with a mix of surprise and reproach in his eyes. But Andras was beyond caring about anyone's feelings; he prayed fervently for the professor to perform like a god and save his beloved An's life.

Andras clutched his head, gazing at the square blocks of the aging hospital with its uniform brick walls. In the campus, amid the blocks, oak trees stood bare, their leaves gone, and their thin branches painted perplexing and somber patterns against the gray sky, heavy with the sound of cold water. Every joint in Andras's body felt on the brink of collapse. He could no longer endure this condition, feeling disconnected from the very essence of life and love. The Danube flowed in silence, the sun concealed its cheerful face behind the somber clouds, and the cold hospital walls remained indifferent to his queries... all of it weighed him down, plunging him into a state of despondency.

He had once confided in An about the art of living truthfully, of cherishing every moment in this world, even the painful ones, for they held their own intrinsic value. Pain, he had told her, was a prerequisite for experiencing true happiness. But now, in this moment of desperation, he felt utterly helpless. Perhaps he had been too arrogant, and now fate had placed him in the most critical of situations. He teetered on the edge, knowing he was about to fall, to lose himself completely, to shatter into pieces. What if An never woke up again? The mere thought of a life without her was unbearable. An, from Hanoi, had given birth to the man he had become today, here in Budapest. When she was by his side, Budapest had been a place of beauty and romance, filled with joy and the fervor of passionate love. But with her gone, the enchantment had vanished, and the flame of life, which once burned so passionately, had flickered out.

***

Professor Hoang Lam placed a glass of cold water before the man from Budapest. Gazing at Andras' countenance, he couldn't help but acknowledge the undeniable handsomeness of this young man. It was no wonder that his fellow countrywoman, An, had declined the professor's enthusiastic invitation. An had refrained from visiting his house, refusing to let him show her around Budapest and Lake Balaton as they had done during their previous dates. An, a renowned young writer in the country, had caught Professor Hoang Lam's attention through her works, which he had read online long before they ever met. Her daring discoveries and paradoxical literary style, reflective of her own lifestyle, had consistently surprised and impressed him. When they finally encountered each other at an international literary conference in Hanoi, he felt an immediate affinity for her. That's when he extended an invitation for her to visit Budapest and experience the reality of a Vietnamese exile who had spent thirty years abroad. She had agreed to visit and stay at his house, but now, due to the presence of this incredibly attractive young man in Budapest, she had postponed their meeting. If he were in An's shoes, he thought he might have acted the same way, forsaking everything to follow such a captivating and handsome gentleman.

Yet now, those charismatic blue eyes were brimming with fear, the chestnut hair hung limply, dimming the radiance that once emanated from his smooth

forehead and arched brows. The layer of stubble on his cheeks, chin, and around his mouth added years of anxiety to his visage. He had once been young, adventurous, and strong, but also reckless and impulsive. Now, he bore the weight of failure, unable to protect the girl he loved more than life itself.

"Andras, fetch some water," the professor finally spoke. But Andras appeared oblivious to the professor's words, his mind lost in a fog of disbelief. The news delivered by the professor seemed like a cocktail of both good and bad tidings. An had regained consciousness, escaping the clutches of Death, but now she faced the grim reality that her leg joints were irreversibly damaged from lying on the ice for too long.

Perhaps Andras had misheard or the old professor was overwhelmed by a nervous breakdown. It couldn't be true that An, his beloved, would lose both her legs! It felt utterly unfair for a spirited nomadic female writer like her, who had traversed the world with joy, penning her adventures. An was the one who required her legs to journey to the ends of the earth—the one who deserved two strong, nimble legs more than anyone else. Or, in this heart-wrenching twist, the envious devil had appeared, disrupting all their plans and desires, altering the course of their destinies according to its whim.

Pop!

Andras startled, jolted from his thoughts as the professor's palm landed heavily on his face, sending him tumbling from his chair. He stood, facing the professor, bitterness seeping through his words.

"Please, slap me again," he implored.

The professor's gaze pierced through his glasses, his words tinged with sorrow. "Never mind. You're awake."

In the midst of this tumultuous moment, the professor urged Andras to be sober, composed, and mentally strong, to support An in overcoming this profound shock. He apologized for the heartache both of them were enduring and acknowledged that words might feel hollow at this juncture. But he reassured Andras that he had done his utmost to save her.

"Thank you, doc," Andras stammered, his emotions raw, "but her legs... we can't just accept this fate."

"Sometimes, tragedies strike, and though we may want to rewrite our lives to alter the circumstances, we can't," the professor replied with wisdom. "We have to accept that which belongs to God and surrender it to Him."

"The devil! Not God..." Andras mumbled in anguish.

"Perhaps it depends on how you perceive it," the professor responded, rising to his feet. He pulled Andras up, peering deep into his dry, anguished blue eyes. "But there's one thing I believe only you can do to save her—love her unconditionally. Stay by her side and offer her your strong legs."

***

Andras knelt by An's hospital bed, his voice soft and tender: "Where's your hand? Let me see your hand," he requested gently.

An hesitated before pulling her hand out from under the thin white blanket, her fragile figure sinking into the mattress. "Are you afraid my hands will be taken apart like my legs?" she questioned with a hint of sadness.

Andras couldn't answer, his throat tightening with emotion. He tried to hold back the tears, but they had already blurred his glasses. With trembling hands, he slipped an engagement ring onto his ring finger—a young maroon gem, the color of their favorites, the color of their souls. He pressed his face into her hand, kissing it, as if seeking solace.

An gazed at him, her black hair cascading on the white pillow. She remained remarkably calm, but tears welled up, betraying her composure. She used her other hand to wipe away the tears, wanting to see him clearly, and she asked:

"The ring is beautiful. But why did you break the Budapest oath? We vowed to be together for the rest of our lives, as lovers, life partners, and confidants, but not in the conventional sense of husband and wife. Has our love changed just because I lost my legs?"

"I don't know how our love will evolve," Andras admitted. "All I know is that I love you more than ever, and I'm afraid. If I leave you even for a few minutes, I'm not sure if I'll ever find you again or if you'll be safe... I'm so confused, and I believe that marriage is the only way to ensure you'll stay with me, body and soul, for all time."

"But I wanted to roam the world..." An gazed out the window, her tears now still.

"And I will carry you around the world. I am your strong legs," Andras vowed. Gently, he lifted her into his arms and walked to the window. He felt a pang of sorrow seeing her light body cradled in his embrace, like a little child. An wrapped her arms around his neck, resting her cheek against his chest. The pain in his heart resonated with hers, tightening the bond between them.

She loved him, but she wouldn't become dependent, leaning on him to climb Géllert Hill. Though she no longer had legs, her body may be imperfect, but her soul was perfect and beautiful—perfectly in sync with his own soul. Their souls were forever soulmates, inspiring each other, co-creating, and elevating one another without the need for physical reliance.

***

Andras had meticulously prepared a romantic wedding ceremony, an unprecedented event in the history of Budapest—a man marrying his beloved in the hospital, on the very day she was discharged. A carpet of white roses adorned the entrance to the hospital treatment area, with their names intertwined in red and pink flowers, forming a heart, bathing the space in a blissful glow. Andras had instructed everyone to keep it a secret, intending to surprise An.

In his formal black suit with a crimson rose pinned to the lapel, Andras nervously brought a pristine white wedding dress into An's hospital room. He had personally chosen the gown, hoping it would fit her petite frame perfectly. In his eyes, she would be the most beautiful princess, his and only his. Overcoming the ordeal of pain they had endured, he believed they had grown even closer, and he loved her more deeply than ever. It was not just love or infatuation—it was a profound worship of her angelic light.

With excitement, Andras halted in front of the empty hospital bed. "Where are you?" he whispered anxiously.

Leaving the white wedding dress on the bed, he rushed to the bathroom, but An was not there. He searched the adjacent room, the corridor, and even Professor Hoang Lam's room in a panic. The professor had to inform him that An had already flown back to Vietnam, a decision he had to respect.

Furious, Andras couldn't believe his meticulously planned surprise had been thwarted. Today was meant to be their wedding day. He was determined to chase after her. He drove to the airport, booked the earliest flight to Vietnam with a connection at Russia's Sheremetyevo airport, and anxiously awaited his departure.

While waiting, he stumbled upon hot news flashing before his eyes—the Russian airline flight, the same one An was on, had crashed upon landing, and only two men survived. His heart pounded in his chest as he read the news again, hoping against hope that An was safe. He could not fathom a world without her— the girl who had transformed his life, filling it with passion, surprises, and a burning love he could not control. He prayed that she was unharmed, even though she had vanished, leaving him in a state of despair.

Did An intentionally bring this upon herself? Andras pondered in the darkness of his thoughts. He remembered how she once whispered to him about her ideal death—an abrupt end on a flight, just one strike, and she would vanish without pain, not even knowing that she had passed away. The idea of dying in a hospital, with surgeons' scalpel cutting into her body, filled her with dread—the painful surgeries, the ominous black door closing her eyes to the world, and the lingering specter of death.

Was it some supernatural force that caused her plane to catch fire on the runway? Andras couldn't shake off these haunting questions. Was her recent accident and hospitalization a way to seek her own demise? His mind swirled with dark speculations.

All his plans for a romantic wedding, trying to bind her to him forever, relying on his legs to keep her close, were now shattered. An had slipped through his fingers, vanishing to an immortal realm, beyond his reach.

He had broken the sacred Budapest oath they had made, and now he had to pay the price. He could never have her entirely, and he would forever endure the pain of chasing her, pursuing her, trying to conquer her—no matter where she was, in this world or another. It was a lifelong journey for kindred souls, not just an existence in the mortal realm, but a bond beyond.

Andras rose from his seat, his steps uncertain and faltering. The world around him crumbled, leaving him lost and bewildered. The waiter's voice broke him from his daze, realizing he had left his belongings on the coffee table, but he couldn't bring himself to return. In that moment, he had been consumed by the ashes of his dreams and hopes. He felt like nothing but ashes—shattered and adrift.

About the Author

KIEU BICH HAU

Kieu Bich Hau, a celebrated Vietnamese writer and cultural ambassador, is a member of the Vietnam Writers' Association. Born in Hung Yen Province, Vietnam, she is a prominent voice in contemporary literature and an active editor for Writer & Life magazine (Vietnam), NEUMA magazine (Romania), and Humanity magazine (Russia).

She has received numerous accolades, including an honorary doctorate from Prodigy Life Academy (USA) for her extraordinary contributions to literature. Recognized internationally, she serves as the Ambassador of Ukiyoto Publisher (Canada) to Vietnam and is the founder and head of Hanoi Female

Translators, promoting literary exchange and empowerment.

With 28 published works spanning prose, poetry, and essays, Kieu Bich Hau's creative achievements have been widely acclaimed. Her works have been translated into 20 languages, including English, Italian, Korean, and French, amplifying Vietnamese literature globally. She has also earned nine prestigious literary awards, such as Literature Award 2007 (Vietnam), the ART Danubius Prize 2022 for fostering Vietnamese-Hungarian cultural ties and the Great Award of Korea 2023 for promoting Vietnamese poetry and prose internationally.

As a cultural representative, she has participated in numerous global literary events, including the ASEAN-China Writers' Forum (2019, China), the International Poetry Festival - Europa in Versi (2023, Italy), the 10th America poetry Festival in New York (2023, USA) and the World Writers' Meet (2024, India), the University of Washington's panel of Postwar Vietnam (2025, USA).

Kieu Bich Hau's storytelling captures profound human experiences, blending Vietnamese traditions with universal themes. Through her tireless efforts as an author, editor, and cultural advocate, she continues to enrich global understanding of Vietnamese literature and culture.

www.ingramcontent.com/pod-product-compliance
Lightning Source LLC
LaVergne TN
LVHW041712070526
838199LV00045B/1315